CONCISE
DICTIONARY OF
PROVERBS

A Perfect Reference for Students of all age groups.
Useful guide for aspirants of IAS, CAT, GMAT,
Civil Services, IELTS, TOEFL & Other Examinations

$\mathcal{V\&S}$ PUBLISHERS

Published by:

V&S PUBLISHERS

F-2/16, Ansari Road, Daryaganj, New Delhi-110002
☎ 011-23240026, 011-23240027 • *Fax* 011-23240028
Email info@vspublishers.com • *Website* www.vspublishers.com

Regional Office Hyderabad
5-1-707/1, Brij Bhawan (Beside Central Bank of India Lane)
Bank Street, Koti, Hyderabad - 500 095
☎ 040-24737290
E-mail vspublishershyd@gmail.com

Branch Office Mumbai
Godown # 34 at The Model Co-Operative Housing, Society Ltd.,
"Sahakar Niwas", Ground Floor, Next to Sobo Central, Mumbai - 400 034
☎ 022-23510736
E-mail vspublishersmum@gmail.com

Follow us on:

All books available at **www.vspublishers.com**

© **Copyright:** *V&S PUBLISHERS*
ISBN 978-93-505714-6-0
Edition 2014

Printed at : Param Offseters Okhla New Delhi-110020

Publisher's Note

Proverb refers to a popular saying that illustrates something such as a basic truth or a practical precept: *Slow and steady wins the race* is a proverb to live by. It is a short popular saying, usually of unknown and ancient origin, that expresses effectively some commonplace truth or useful thought, adage. For example, *Antarctica is a proverb for extreme cold.* A proverb is a phrase that people use in particular situations; *pardon the expression.*

Considering the growing importance of English in all spheres of life, we recently published an EXC-EL Series (Excellence in English Language) composed of four books - English Vocabulary Made Easy, English Grammar & Usage, Spoken English, and Improve Your Vocabulary. We thought we have done our bit. No sooner, the Series hit the market; a volley of readers sought our help to improve diction, presentation and attractiveness of their conversation – both in writing and speaking.

Being aware that our existence as a publishing house depends solely upon fulfilling readers' expectations and continued patronage, we decided to come out with something that can add spark to any conversation while making it appear interesting. This Dictionary of Proverbs is the outcome. There are three more companion dictionaries on – Idioms, Phrases and Metaphors & Similes.

This book explains the meaning behind hundreds of proverbs that you hear or read in English each day. *The meanings are shown in italics.* In order to keep it concise, this dictionary attempts to present most commonly used proverbs. Having an exhaustive one will just overwhelm you with thousands of proverbs that nobody uses anymore. English remains immensely popular, attractive, articulate and rich language but its proverbs are sometimes 'tough nuts to crack'.

What led us to publish this? Proverbs appear in every language, and English has thousands of them. They are often confusing because the meaning of the whole group of words taken together has little, often nothing, to do with the meaning of the words taken one by one. In order to understand a language, you must be aware of what the proverbs in that language mean. If you try to figure out the meaning of a proverb literally, word by word, you will get completely befuddled.

We would be happy to have your views and comments for improving the content and quality of the edition.

Introduction

Proverbs *are often borrowed from similar languages and cultures, and sometimes come down to the present through more than one language. Both the Bible (including, but not limited to the Book of Proverbs) and medieval Latin (aided by the work of Erasmus) have played a considerable role in distributing proverbs across Europe, although almost every culture has examples of its own.* **A Proverb** *is a simple and concrete saying, popularly known and repeated, that expresses a truth based on common sense or the practical experience of humanity. They are often metaphorical. A proverb that describes a basic rule of conduct may also be known as a maxim.*

Following is a list of Proverbs and their Meanings. Read, understand and learn them as they may be of great help in your day-to-day conversations and in making sentences as well as in writing good English

(A) nimble sixpence is better than a slow shilling. A capable person, even if he is slow or not well qualified, is more valuable than an inefficient person who may be highly qualified

(It is) never too late to repent. It is never too late to say you are sorry, and to change your ways

(One is) never too old to learn. There is no age limit to acquiring knowledge

(The) meek shall inherit the earth. The humble and the downtrodden but not the proud or the mighty will be rewarded with the best at the end of time

(The) race is to the swift. People who are able to overcome life's troubles quickly or do things quickly have the advantage over others

A

A bad excuse is better than none

It is better to give a poor or implausible excuse—which may, in fact, be believed—than to have no explanation or justification at all.

A bad penny always turns up

Undesirable people will always return; often used when somebody who has left in disgrace reappears after a long absence.

A bad tree does not yield good apples

A bad parent brings up bad children.

A bad workman blames his tools

To blame one's equipments instead of taking charge for one's own lack of skills.

A bad workman quarrels with his tools

Workers who lack skill or competence blame their tools or equipment when things go wrong.

A believer is a songless bird in a cage

Religious belief restricts a person's freedom of action and expression.

A bellowing cow soon forgets her calf

The loudest laments or complaints are often the first to subside; used specifically of those whose mourning seems excessive.

A big tree attracts the woodman's axe

Great people attract great criticism.

A bird in hand is worth two in the bush.

Don't risk losing what you already have by running after something better.

A bleating sheep loses a bite

Those who talk too much may miss an important opportunity.

A blind man's wife needs no Paint

Attempts to improve the appearance of somebody or something are superfluous when it is the true nature of the person or thing that is of value, or when the improvements will not be appreciated.

A bribe will enter without knocking

The use of money enables access where it would otherwise be denied.

A broken friendship may be soldered but will never be sound

A friendship is never the same after a fight.

A burden of one's own choice is not felt

Difficult tasks seem easier when done voluntarily.

A burnt child dreads fire

A bad experience or a horrifying incident may scar one's attitude or thinking for a lifetime.

A cat can look at a king

Even the lowliest people have the right to look at, or show an interest in, those of higher status or prestige; often used by somebody accused of staring insolently.

A cat has nine lives

Cats can survive many accidents because they are known to land on their feet and avoid injury.

A cat in gloves catches no mice

It is sometimes necessary to be bold or ruthless, or to do unpleasant things, in order to achieve one's ends.

A cat may look at a king

Anyone has the right to look at or speak to anyone else without having to worry about status, position, upbringing etc.

A chain is no stronger than its weakest link

The success of a group or team depends on the full commitment of every member

A change is as good as a rest

Doing something different for a time can be just as refreshing as taking a break from work; also used more generally of any change in routine.

A chicken and egg question

A mysterious question which can't be answered.

A closed mouth catches no flies

It is better not to say anything than to say something that might get you into trouble.

A coin of gold is delighting in a bag of silver coins

A unique person is praised more.

A constant guest is never welcome

We are apt to grow to dislike friends who visit us too often

A contented mind is a perpetual feast

Contentment of mind is the cause of lasting happiness.

A coward dies a thousand times before his death

The valiant never taste of death but once: brave people don't fear anything while cowards are always pessimistic about outcomes in life.

A creaking door hangs longest

Those who have many minor ailments and infirmities often outlive those who don't.

A dog that will fetch a bone will carry a bone

Beware of people who bring you gossip about others, because they are equally likely to pass on gossip about you.

A dose of adversity is often as needful as a dose of medicine

Hardship and misfortune may be unpleasant, but they can sometimes have a beneficial effect on the character, especially when people fail to appreciate the good things they have.

A dripping June sets all in tune

A rainy June means there will be a good harvest of crops and flowers later in the summer.

A drowning man will clutch at a straw

A desperate person will do anything to save himself.

A dry March, a wet April and a cool May fill barn and cellar and bring much hay

Signifies that harvest predictions are made according to the weather.

A dwarf on a giant's shoulders sees further of the two

Those who build on the breakthroughs of their predecessors surpass their achievements.

A fat kitchen makes a lean will

Those who eat well all their lives will have little money left when they die.

A fault confessed is half redressed

Confession marks the beginning of forgiveness.

A fish stinks from the head

A corrupting influence often spreads from a leader to the rest of the organization or group.

A flower blooms more than once

An occasion missed is available later too.

A fool and his money are soon parted

A person who spends his money foolishly carelessly will soon be penniless

A fool at forty is a fool indeed

People who have not gained the wisdom of experience by the time they reach middle age are likely to remain fools for the rest of their lives

A fool may give a wise man counsel

People are often able to give good advice to those who are considered to be intellectually superior; sometimes said apologetically by the giver of such advice, or used as a warning against disregarding it.

A fool's bolt is soon shot

Foolish people act hastily and thus waste their efforts.

A foolish consistency is the hobgoblin of little minds

A lack of flexibility in making judgments is regarded as a sign of petty narrow-mindedness.

A fox smells its own stink first

A person knows the place they belong in and s/he also knows his/her mistakes.

A friend in need is a friend indeed

A real friend is someone who helps you when you are in trouble.

A friend to all is a friend to none

A person who makes himself close to everyone probably cannot be trusted by any one

A friend's eye is a good mirror

A true and real friend will tell you the truth.

A golden key can open any door

With money you can gain access to anything you want; used specifically of bribery, or more generally of the power and influence of wealth.

A good beginning makes a good end

A well-planned task will be well done.

A good beginning makes a good ending

Something that starts off right will probably succeed all the way and end on the right note

A good conscience is a soft pillow

A guiltless conscience gives one peace of mind.

A good dog deserves a good bone

A loyal servant or employee deserves his reward.

A good example is the best sermon

Providing (being) a good example is better than giving advice.

A good face is a letter of recommendation

An honest demeanor may be interpreted as a sign of a person's integrity.

A good horse cannot be of a bad color

Superficial appearances do not affect the essential worth of something.

A good Jack makes a good Jill

People who live or work together should set a good example to each other—a good husband will have a good wife, a good master will have a good servant, and so on.

A good name is better than precious ointment

Your good name should be your most cherished possession.

A good name is better than riches

A good reputation is precious, difficult to earn and cannot be bought

A good name is sooner lost than won

It takes a long time to build up a good reputation which can be easily destroyed by misconduct.

A good tale is not the worse for being told twice

There is no harm in telling a good joke or anecdote—or a story with a moral—a second time; often used by way of apology or justification for such repetition.

A goose quill is more dangerous than a lion's claw

Written words of criticism or defamation can do more harm or cause more pain than a physical attack.

A great book is a great evil

A long book is a bad book—good writers know how to express themselves concisely.

A great city, a great solitude

People often feel more lonely in a large city, among thousands of strangers, than they would do if they were actually alone.

A great talker is a great liar

A smooth and persuasive talker may be a good liar.

A growing youth has a wolf in his stomach

Adolescent boys are perpetually hungry.

A guilty conscience needs no accuser

If one knows that one has committed a wrongdoing, one won't need anyone to tell one that one is guilty.

A heavy purse makes a light heart

Those who have plenty of money are happy and carefree.

A horse can't pull while kicking

People engaged in acts of insubordination or protest cannot work efficiently or productively.

A house divided against itself cannot stand

Discord breaks up families.

A house without books is like a room without windows

Books brighten and enlighten our daily lives in the same way that windows brighten and illuminate a room.

A hungry belly has no ears

A hungry person will only concentrate on their hunger and desire for food.

A hungry stomach has no ears

There is no point in talking to or reasoning with hungry people, or those who are greedily devouring their food.

A hungry wolf is fixed to no place

A desperate person will go anywhere to satisfy his/her needs.

A jack of all trades is master of none

Somebody who has a very wide range of abilities or skills usually does not excel at any of them.

A jackass can kick a barn door down, but it takes a carpenter to build one

Something that has taken time, skill, and effort to put together can be quickly ruined or destroyed by a foolish person.

A job worth doing is a job worth doing well

When you do something you should do it as well as you can.

A journey of a thousand miles begins with a single step

To succeed at anything, you first need to get started

A leopard can't change its spots

A person's character cannot be changed very easily (especially if it is a bad character).

A leopard cannot change its spots

A person's nature cannot change.

A liar is worse than a thief

People who lie are even less trustworthy than people who thieve.

A lie begets a lie

One lie leads to another.

A lie can go around the world and back again while the truth is lacing up its boots

False rumors travel with alarming speed.

A light purse makes a heavy heart

We cannot be cheerful when we have financial problems.

A little absence does much good

A short period of absence can have a surprisingly beneficial effect.

A little fire is quickly trodden out

If a small problem is dealt with quickly, it will not turn into a major issue.

A little knowledge is a dangerous thing

Knowing only a little about something can cause you to distort the truth or overestimate, misunderstand something

A little pot is soon hot

Small people are reputed to be more easily angered than others.

A loaded wagon makes no noise

People who are wealthy do not talk about money.

A loveless life is living death

Life is difficult without affection.

A man can die but once

Death only occurs once.

A man can only die once

Death can only happen once in a lifetime.

A man is a lion in his own cause

People tend to exceed expectations when they have a personal interest in something.

A man is as old as he feels himself to be

One's age doesn't matter as long as one is fit and healthy.

A man is as old as he feels

A person is old only if s/he feels old. Age is just a number; it has nothing to do with a person's actions.

A man is known by the company he keeps

You can tell about a person by observing who he spends time with

A man is ruled by his passions

Your character, personality, attitude etc can be overtaken by your emotions if they are strong enough

A man who is his own lawyer has a fool for his client

It is not wise to act as your own attorney in a court of law, or in some other legal process; also used in other fields of activity requiring professional expertise or objectivity.

A man wrapped up in himself makes a very small bundle

Self-centeredness is not a quality that is associated with greatness.

A man's got to do what a man's got to do

You must do what needs to be done, or what you feel ought to be done, however unpleasant it may be; sometimes used facetiously.

A man's home is his castle

People have the right to privacy and freedom of action in their own home.

A man's word is as good as his bond

Honorable people do not break their promises.

A man's home is his castle

You feel most secure, free and in control in your own home

A mind is a terrible thing to waste

one's intelligence should not be wasted mindlessly.

A miss is as good as a mile

What one already has is better than something that one may not be able to obtain.

A monkey in silk is a monkey no less

No matter how someone dresses, it's the same person underneath.

A mouse may help a lion

Small or lowly people can sometimes give valuable assistance to those who are greater or more powerful than themselves

A new broom sweeps clean

A newly-appointed person makes quick changes.

A nod is as good as a wink

A hint or suggestion can be accepted and acted upon without further elaboration.

A nod's as good as a wink to a blind horse

In certain circumstances only the smallest hint is needed to make yourself understood; also used to imply that any kind of hint is wasted on somebody who is determined not to take it

A postern door makes a thief

It is all too easy to rob a house that has a rear entrance through which people can slip in and out unnoticed

A pot of milk is ruined by a drop of poison

Something bad no matter how small can ruin all your plans, successes etc.

A problem shared is a problem halved

A problem when discussed with someone becomes easier to solve.

A prophet is not without honor, save in his own country

People who give words of warning or wisdom are not heeded or appreciated by those closest to them

A reed before the wind lives on, while mighty oaks do fall

Those who are flexible and relatively insignificant can survive crises that bring down more prominent people who are unable or unwilling to yield or adapt

A rising tide lifts all boats

Refers to something that is helpful to all.

A rolling stone gathers no moss

Constant movement does not provide a person with any sort of possession, be it material or emotional.

A rose by any other name would smell just as sweet

It is not what a thing is called that matters, but what it is.

A rotten apple spoils the barrel.

A single immoral person can have a bad influence on the entire group.

A short horse is soon curried

A small job is finished quickly.

A small gift usually gets small thanks

Give people less than they expect and they will be less grateful to you.

A small leak will sink a great ship

Small problems are worth the time to fix as they can eventually cause great damage

A smooth sea never made a skilled mariner

Overcoming adversity leads to competence.

A smooth sea never made a skilled mariner

Overcoming troubles leads to improvement of one's abilities.

A son is a son till he gets him a wife, a daughter's a daughter all of her life

Men may neglect one's parents after he gets married but a daughter will always maintain her love for them, even after getting married.

A stitch in time saves nine

Dealing with a problem at an early stage will save time. It'll prevent it from getting worse.

A straw will show which way the wind blows

A small incident can unravel a significant event.

A stumble may prevent a fall.

Correct a small mistake and it may help one avoid making a bigger one.

A swallow does not make the summer

One good event does not mean that everything is alright.

A tale never loses in the telling

People exaggerate a story a little each time it is retold.

A thing of beauty is a joy forever

The memory of something beautiful will last forever.

A thing you don't want is dear at any price

Do not be tempted to buy something you do not need just because it is cheap.

A traveler may lie with authority
People who have traveled may boast of their experiences without fear of contradiction.

A tree is known by its fruit
A person is judged by their actions.

A trouble shared is a trouble halved
Sharing your problem with someone will make it easier to handle and solve it.

A watched pot never boils
It seems that things take longer to happen when you watch or wait with impatience.

A wet May brings plenty of hay
Wet weather in May means the hay harvest will be good later in the year.

A wise man changes his mind sometimes, a fool never
It is wise to reconsider your plans, ideas, actions in the light of new information rather than to blindly stick to an earlier decision

A word spoken is past recalling
What has been said cannot be taken back, so think before you speak

A word to the wise is enough
You need not be long-winded when speaking to intelligent people or those who understand you well

A young barber and an old physician
Youth is fine in a barber but undesirable in a doctor.

A young idler, an old beggar
If you don't work when you are young, you won't have any money for when you're old.

A young man married is a young man marred
It is not good to marry too young.

Absence is the mother of disillusion
Separation makes one consider in a different and probably, less favourable way.

Absence makes the heart grow fonder
When you are away from someone you love, you tend to love them even more.

Accidents will happen in the best-regulated families
No amount of carefulness will ensure against accidents or mistakes.

Accidents will happen
Some unfortunate events are inevitable.

Action is worry's worst enemy
You can banish anxiety by keeping busy and active, or by taking action to solve the problem that is worrying you

Actions speak louder than words
What a person actually does matters more than what they say they will do.

Admiration is the daughter of ignorance
People often admire others about whom they only have incomplete knowledge.

Adventures are to the adventurous
not taking risks will ensure that one has a boring and unspectacular life.

Adversity makes strange bedfellows
People who share the same misfortune are drawn together.

Advice is cheap
It doesn't cost anything to offer advice.

Advice is least heeded when most needed
When a problem is serious, people often do not follow the advice given.

Advice most needed is least heeded
People tend to ignore or overlook the help or advice they nee the most

Advisors run no risks
It's easier to give advice than to act upon a problem.

After a storm, comes a calm
Every problem eventually comes to an end, so cheer up

After death the doctor
Help sometimes comes too late

After dinner rest a while, after supper walk a mile
It is best for digestion to rest after a heavy meal and exercise after a light meal.

Age before beauty
Older people have precedence over those who are younger and more attractive; said when standing back to let another person go first or when pushing in ahead of somebody

Alcohol will preserve anything but a secret
People tend to talk freely and indiscreetly when under the influence of alcohol.

All animals are equal, but some are more equal than others
Everybody may seem equal in a society, but there are always some who are dominant to others.

All cats are grey in the dark
People are the same as each other until they individually make a name for themselves.

All covet, all lose
Trying to obtain everything will lead one to risk losing everything.

All days are short to industry and long to idleness
Time proceeds slowly when one is idle.

All for one and one for all
People who are committed to working together for a positive outcome

All good things come to an end
Every event, no matter how enjoyable, must end at some point

All good things come to those who wait
Patience is always rewarded.

All men are created equal
Every human is built the same and therefore, everybody is equal.

All roads lead to Rome
There are different ways to reach one objective.

All that glitters is not gold
Appearances can be deceptive.

All the world loves a lover
Everyone loves to see people in love

All things are difficult before they are easy
everything becomes easier with practice.

All things come to him who waits
You will get what you want if you are willing to wait for it patiently

All things grow with time - except grief
Grief lessens with time.

All words are pegs to hang ideas on
Words are used to formulate and communicate ideas.

All work and no play makes Jack a dull boy

It is not good to work all the time. One needs to relax.

All's for the best in the best of all possible worlds

Referring to universal optimism that everything can be as good as it is right now.

All's fair in love and war

Where powerful emotions are concerned, there can be no firm rules of behavior

All's fish that comes the net

When something comes our way we should consider how it might be useful or benefit us.

All's well that ends well

A happy ending to a difficult situation can help you forget or disregard the earlier trouble

Always in a hurry, always behind

Trying to do things quickly will cause that job to be done badly.

An apple a day keeps the doctor away

A small method of prevention will keep one guarded against bigger health problems.

An army marches on its stomach.

You must eat well if you want to work effectively or achieve great things.

An empty bag will not stand upright

Quality comes with effort

An empty purse frightens away friends.

Friends disappear when one does not have monetary possessions.

An empty sack cannot stand upright

People who are poor or hungry cannot survive, work effectively, or remain honest.

An Englishman's home is his castle

A man's home is equal to his castle because he feels secure and at peace there.

An hour in the morning is worth two in the evening

People are at their most efficient early in the day, when they are refreshed by sleep.

An idle brain is the devil's workshop

Idleness leads one to unwanted temptations.

An old fox is not easily snared

A person with years of experience is unlikely to be easily fooled.

An old poacher makes the best gamekeeper

A reformed wrongdoer is good at preventing others from committing the same crime or offense, because he or she can understand their thinking and anticipate their actions.

An open door may tempt a saint

It is best not to put temptation in anybody's way—even the most honest and upright person might find it hard to resist.

An ounce of common sense is worth a pound of theory

A practical commonsense approach is often far more effective than abstract theorizing

An ounce of discretion is worth a pound of pit

Good judgment is often more

valuable than knowledge or learning; also interpreted more literally as a warning to tactfully refrain from making jokes at another's expense

An ounce of prevention is worth a pound of cure

It is easier to prevent something in the beginning than to face the repercussions later.

And at the end is mild

Anger improves nothing but the arch of a cat's back: nothing is gained by losing one's temper

Anger is the one thing made better by delay

Do not to speak or act immediately when angry.

Anger without power is folly

Don't get angry about things you can't do anything about.

Any time means no time

Unplanned and vague events will never happen.

Appearances are deceptive

What looks good may not really be so

Appetite comes with eating

Desire or enthusiasm for something often increases as you do it.

April showers bring May flowers

Unpleasant things in the present may give good results in the future.

Art is long and life is short

Works of art last longer than human lives.

As a tree falls, so shall it lie

People should not attempt to change their beliefs or opinions just because they are about to die.

As good be an addled egg as an idle bird

Somebody who tries and fails has achieved no less than somebody who does nothing at all; used as a reprimand for idleness or inaction.

As Maine goes, so goes the nation

Members of a group will follow the most influential person of that group.

As soon as a man is born, he begins to die

Death is the destiny of every man

As the day lengthens, so the cold strengthens

The coldest part of the winter often occurs in the period following the shortest day, as the hours of daylight begin to grow longer.

As the twig is bent, so is the tree inclined

A child's early education and training are of great importance in determining the way he or she will grow up.

As you bake, so shall you brew

The way you begin determines whether you will do badly or well

As you brew, so shall you drink

People have to face the consequences of their actions

As you make your bed so must you lie on it

You must accept the consequences of your act.

As you sow, so shall you reap

You should accept the consequences of your actions.

Ask a silly question and you get a silly answer

A stupid question will get an obvious and sarcastic answer.

Ask me no questions and I'll tell you no lies

It is better not to ask questions that somebody is likely to be unwilling to answer truthfully; used in response to such a question or simply to discourage an inquisitive person.

Ask no questions and hear no lies

Do not force a person into telling you a lie by forcing him to talk about something he does not want to talk about

Avoid evil and it will avoid thee

Stay out of trouble, and trouble will not follow you

Avoidance is the only remedy

Some-times the only solution to a problem is toavoid it in the first place

Away goes the devil when he finds the door shut against him

Evil will never triumph if all temptations are rejected.

B

Bad money drives out good

The existence or availability of something inferior or worthless—whether it be money, music, literature, or whatever—has a tendency to make things of better quality or greater value more scarce

Bad is never good until worse happens

A bad situation you have been complaining about will suddenly seem a blessing when something worse happens

Bad money drives out good

The existence or availability of something inferior or worthless—whether it be money, music, literature, or whatever—has a tendency to make things of better quality or greater value more scarce.

Bad news travels fast

People seem to hear bad news very fast

Barking dogs seldom bite

Those who make loud threats seldom carry them out.

Be careful what you wish for, you might just get it

What you wish for may not really be what is good for you.

Be just before you're generous.

You should make sure all your debts are paid and other obligations met before you start giving money away or living extravagantly.

Be kind to your friends; if it weren't for them, you would be a total stranger

You cannot afford to lose your friends by treating them badly, because without them you would be alone in society

Be swift to hear, slow to speak

One should listen carefully before speaking.

Be the day weary or be the day long, at last it ringeth to evensong

No matter how tiring or stressful a day you are having, you can console yourself with the fact that it will eventually be over; (also used more generally to recommend perseverance or endurance in a trying situation).

Bear and forbear

Patience, tolerance, endurance, and forgiveness are valuable qualities in all walks of life.

Beauty and honesty seldom agree

It is rare for a person to be both good-looking and honest.

Beauty draws with a single hair.

A beautiful woman has great powers of attraction.

Beauty is a good letter of introduction

Beautiful people make a better first impression on strangers than ugly people do.

Beauty is but a blossom

Good looks do not last

Beauty is in the eye of the beholder.

The perception of beauty is subjective, and not everybody finds the same people or things attractive.

Beauty is no inheritance

Good looks are not necessarily passed on from generation-to-generation.

Beauty is only skin deep

Beauty is only a superficial quality, and may conceal an unpleasant character or nature.

Beauty is truth, truth beauty

The qualities of beauty and truth are, or should be, inseparable and interlinked; often used when real life falls short of this ideal.

Before criticizing a man, walk a mile in his shoes

Do not criticize a person without understanding his/her situation.

Beggars can't be choosers

Someone in need should be grateful for what is given to him —even if it's not what he wants or expects.

Behind every great man is a great woman

Important or successful men often owe their status or success to the support of a female partner or colleague.

Believing has a core of unbelieving

Belief and unbelief are closely related, and sometimes you need to start from a position of skepticism to arrive at the truth.

Better a big fish in a little pond than a little fish in a big pond

It is better to have a position of importance in a small organization than to be an unimportant member of a large group.

Better a dinner of herbs where love is than a stalled ox where hate is

It is better to be poor or dine badly in a loving environment than to eat well or have a wealthy lifestyle in an atmosphere of discord or hatred.

Better a good cow than a cow of a good

A person's character is of more importance than his or her family background.

Better a little fire to warm us than a big one to burn us

Sometimes it is more desirable to have only a small amount of something.

Better a mouse in the pot than no meat at all

To have something, no matter how little or poor in quality, is better than to have nothing at all.

Better an egg today than a hen tomorrow

It is preferable to have something that is sure now than looking for the possibility of something that may occur later.

Better be alone than in bad company

Be careful in the choice of your acquaintances.

Better be safe than sorry

It is wise to take precautions rather than be upset that you did not prepare for an eventuality after something has happened

Better be the head of a dog than the tail of a lion

It's better to be the leader of a small group than to be secondary in a bigger one.

Better be untaught than ill-taught

It's better not to be taught at all than to be taught badly.

Better flatter a fool than fight him

Avoid disputes with stupid people.

Better late than never

To do something that is right, profitable, or good a little late is still better than not doing it at all.

Better late than never.

Do something, even if it's late, rather than not doing it at all.

Better lose the saddle than the horse

It's better to stop and accept a small loss than continue and risk losing everything.

Better one house spoiled than two

It is a good thing for two bad, foolish, or otherwise undesirable people to become husband and wife and thus avoid causing trouble in two separate marriages.

Better safe than sorry

It's better to be too careful.

Better the devil you know than the devil you don't know

It is often preferable to choose or stay with people or things you know, despite their faults, than to risk replacing them with somebody or something new but possibly less desirable.

Better to be alone than in bad company

It is better to be by yourself than to be with people who are a bad influence

Better to die with honor than live with shame

It is more honorable to do the right thing even if you will be punished or have to die for it than to live as a coward or a liar

Better to drink the milk than to eat the cow

Be careful not to destroy the source of your income.

Between a rock and a hard place

Trapped in a difficult situation, with no means of escape.

Between the devil and the deep sea

To choose between two equally bad alternatives in a serious dilemma.

Beware of an oak, it draws the stroke; avoid an ash, it counts the flash; creep under the thorn, it can save you from harm

It is dangerous to shelter from lightning under the oak, ash, or other trees.

Beware of Greeks bearing gifts

It is wise to be suspicious of offers or friendly gestures made by enemies or opponents.

Birds in their little nests agree

People who live or work together should try to do so in harmony; often used to stop children from arguing.

Birds of a feather flock together

People tend to associate with those of similar character, interests, or opinions; often used with derogatory implications.

Birth is much but breeding more

A person's upbringing counts for more in the long run than the traits of character he or she was born with.

Bite off more than one can chew

To try to do something one is unable to do.

Bitter pills may have blessed effects

Something may be unpleasant or painful, but it can help you in the long run

Blessings brighten as they take their flight

People often fail to appreciate the good things that they have until they lose them.

Blood is thicker than water

Family ties are stronger than any other.

Blood will have blood

One act of violence provokes another, by way of revenge. (blood will tell Inherited characteristics— whether good or bad—cannot be hidden forever).

Books and friends should be few but good

You do not need to have too many friends or read too many books in order to live a balanced, fulfilled and complete life as long as the friends and books you do have are full of substance.

Boys will be boys

Often applied to men who act childishly. Boys must be forgiven for their bad or boisterous behavior; also used ironically when grown men behave in an irresponsible or childish manner.

Brain is better than brawn

Intelligence is more valuable than physical strength

Bread always falls buttered-side down

Of two possibilities, it often seems that the more negative one will occur

Brevity is the soul of wit

When you want to sound clever, it is better to be brief rather than long-winded

Burn not your house to scare away the mice.

Do not try to solve a minor problem by taking action that will cause much greater harm.

Burn the candle at both ends

Those who are always busy and seem to get little rest

Business before pleasure

It is better to finish your work before you have a good time

Busy folks are always meddling

It is in the nature of busy people to interfere in the affairs of others.

Buy a pig in a poke

Buy something without examining it for faults or checking to see if they are really getting what they believe they have purchased

By timely mending save much spending

Fix a problem as soon as you discover it to save money, expense, worry, etc having to deal with it later when it has become a bigger problem

C

Caesar's wife must be above suspicion

Those in positions of importance— and their associates—must lead blameless lives and have spotless reputations.

Calamity is the touchstone of a brave mind

It is at times of crisis that you find out who the truly strong, courageous, or great people are.

Call a man a thief and he will steal

Give a person a bad reputation and he or she may start to justify it.

Call a spade a spade

Identify things by their real names; do not prevaricate about awkward truths; say what you mean.

Care is no cure

Worrying about something does nothing to put it right.

Catch as catch can

To do anything or use any means to achieve an aim or reach a goal.

Catch not at the shadow and lose the substance

We should not waste time on trivial aspects of a matter and neglect the essential matter itself.

Catch not at the shadow and lose the substance

Do not allow yourself to be distracted from your main purpose by irrelevancies.

Catching's before hanging

Offenders can only be punished when or if they are caught.

Chance favors the prepared mind

You should always be prepared to act so that when opportunities present themselves, you are ready to seize them

Charity begins at home

A person's first obligation should be to help the member of his own family before he can begin thinking of talking about helping others.

Charity begins at home

A person's first duty is to help and care for his/her own family.

Charity is not a bone you throw to a dog but a bone you share with a dog

There should be more to charity than simply giving money or other material goods—it is better to

24

establish a relationship with those in need and to work with them for the benefit of all concerned.

Cheapest is dearest

Some items may save you money because they are cheap, but their quality may be poor, and this may cost you a lot of money in repairs and getting replacements later

Children and fools speak the truth

Children and foolish people have a tendency to say what is true, because they have not learned that it may be advantageous or diplomatic to do otherwise.

Children are certain cares, but uncertain comforts

Children are bound to cause their parents anxiety, and may or may not also bring them joy.

Children should be seen and not heard

To stop a child from asking questions, talking, or making unnecessary noise.

Christmas comes but once a year

Extravagance and self-indulgence at Christmas—or any other annual celebration—can be justified by the fact that it is a relatively infrequent occurrence.

Christmas comes but once each year

An excuse to indulge in food and drink and spend money during the Christmas season.

Circumstances alter cases

The same general principle cannot be applied to every individual case, and what is right, good, or appropriate in one set of circumstances may be wrong in another.

Cleanliness is next to Godliness

To be clean and tidy is equally important as being spiritually good and religious.

Clothes make the man

The way you dress tells people something about you, and can influence their opinion of you

Coming events cast their shadows before

Future events, especially those of some significance, can often be predicted from the warning signs that precede them.

Common fame is seldom to blame

Rumors are rarely without substance, and if unpleasant things are being said about somebody, then that person has probably done something to deserve them.

Comparisons are odious

It is bad to compare people to one another

Confess and be hanged

There is little incentive for confession when punishment is the inevitable result; used as justification for not owning up to wrongdoing.

Confessed faults are half-mended

When you own up to a fault, mistake or wrongdoing, you are halfway to changing into a better person

Conscience gets a lot of credit that belongs to cold feet

Something commended as an act of conscience may be simply due to cowardice or loss of nerve.

Constant occupation prevents temptation.

Work allows one to avoid temptation.

Councils of war never fight

When a number of people get together to discuss something important, they rarely decide on a drastic course of action.

Courage is fear that has said its prayers

A brave person is not necessarily fearless, but has drawn strength from religion or some other source.

Courtesy costs nothing

Politeness should be a way of life for everyone

Courtesy is contagious

If you are polite to other people, then they will be polite to you.

Cowards die many deaths

A coward is afraid of everything, and therefore, faces every problem or challenge with great fear

Cream always comes to the top

People of great worth or quality will ultimately enjoy high achievement or public recognition.

Crime does not pay

However much you may earn or make as a criminal, a life of crime does not pay because the law will catch up with you eventually; Criminal activity may seem to be profitable, at least in the short term, but it ultimately leads to far greater loss—of liberty, or even of life;used as a deterrent slogan.

Crime must be concealed by crime

One crime often leads to another, committed to avoid detection of the first.

Cross the stream where it is shallowest

Always take the easiest possible approach to doing something.

Cross the stream where it is shallowest

Don't make things difficult for yourself; always find the simplest means of achieving your objective.

Crosses are ladders that lead to heaven

Suffering and misfortune often bring out the best in a person's character.

Cry over spilled milk

It's pointless to get upset or feel regret about a loss or mistake that can't be undone

Curiosity killed the cat

To warn people not to show too much interest in affairs that don't concern them.

Curses are like chickens, they come home to roost

Curses you place on others may

find their fulfilment in you, so it is best not to curse anyone

Curses, like chickens, come home to roost

Wrongdoers ultimately have to suffer the consequences of their bad deeds;also used when those who have wished evil on others are struck by misfortune themselves.

Cut off your nose to spite your face

When people are dissatisfied or angry, they sometimes react by doing foolish things that prove harmful to themselves.

Cut your coat according to your cloth

Live within your income; don't be too ambitious in your plans.

D

Danger and delight grow on the same stalk

Some pleasures will lead you to danger

Dead men don't bite

A dead person can no longer do others any harm; often used to justify murder.

Dead men tell no lies

A dead person cannot reveal secrets and cause problems.

Dead men tell no tales

It may be expedient to kill somebody who could betray a secret or give information about the criminal activities of others.

Death is the great leveler

People of all ranks and classes are equal in death, and nobody is exempt from dying.

Deeds are fruits, words are but leaves

Taking action is far better than just talking about problems or negative situations

Desert and reward seldom keep company

People are often not rewarded for their good deeds or meritorious behavior; conversely, those who do receive rewards have often done nothing to deserve them.

Desperate diseases must have desperate remedies

Drastic action is called for— and justified—when you find yourself in a particularly difficult situation.

Desperate times call for desperate measures

Sometimes, a situation is so urgent or unexpected that you have to resort to doing things you normally would not

Diamonds cut diamonds

Refers to two people who are equally witty.

Different strokes for different folks

Every individual has different opinions, ideas and preferences.

Different strokes for different talks

You need different plans or strategies in managing different people as people are different in personality and temperament

Diligence is the mother of good fortune

Hard work gives rewards.

Discretion is the better part of valor

It is often wiser to avoid taking an unnecessary risk than to be recklessly courageous.

Diseases of the soul are more dangerous than those of the body

Mental and emotional problems

are more painful than physical wounds.

Distance lends enchantment to the view

When you are free of a problem or far away from troublesome people, you begin to feel that things were not so bad after all

Distance makes the heart grow fonder

Separation from the person one loves strengthens one's feelings for them.

Divide and rule

A method of ruling or managing people where you separate them into different groups to make sure they do not join forces against you

Do as I saw, and not as I do

Do something as you have seen it done although it may be different from your own way of doing it

Do not cross a bridge till you come to it

Do not worry about something before it has happened

Do not have too many irons in the fire

If we attempt to do too much at once, we shall not do anything properly

Do not ride the high horse

Do not be arrogant

Do unto others as you would others do unto you

Treat others as you would like them to treat you.

Doctors make the worst patients

It is difficult advising people on matters they are supposed to be experts on because they believe they know better

Dog eat dog

In competitive situations where each person has his own interests at heart, it is usually the strong and the determined who succeed.

Don't bite the hand that feeds you

Do not behave unkindly or ungratefully toward those on whom you depend for financial or other support.

Don't burn your bridges

Don't behave in such a manner that you have no chance of turning back to safety.

Don't cry before you're hurt

There is no point in upsetting yourself about something bad that may or may not happen.

Don't cry over spilt milk

Don't worry about and regret things that have occurred in the past.

Don't cut off your nose to spite your face

Do not take action to spite others that will harm you more than them.

Don't cut off your nose to spite your face don't interfere in others' problems

Don't get mad, get even Take positive action to retaliate for a wrong that has been done to you, rather than wasting your time and energy in angry recriminations.

Don't hide your light under a bushel

If you have special skills or talents, do not conceal them through modesty and prevent others from appreciating or benefiting from them.

Don't let the fox guard the hen house

Do not put somebody in a position where he or she will be tempted to wrongdoing.

Don't overload gratitude; if you do, she'll kick

When people are grateful to you, do not take excessive advantage of the situation, because any sense of obligation has its limits.

Don't put the cart before the horse

It is important to do things in the right or natural order; also used when people confuse cause and effect.

Don't shout until you are out of the woods

Avoid any show of triumph or relief until you are sure that a period of difficulty or danger is over.

Don't take down a fence unless you are sure why it was put up

Most things were constructed or established for a purpose, and it is unwise to destroy or dismantle them unless you are certain that they are not longer required.

Don't talk the talk if you can't walk the walk

Don't boast of something if you are unwilling or unable to back it up by your actions.

Don't teach your grandmother to suck eggs

Do not presume to give advice or instruction to those who are older and more experienced than you.

Don't throw good money after bad

If you have already spent money on a venture that seems likely to fail, do not waste any further money on it.

Don't throw out the baby with the bathwater

Do not take the drastic step of abolishing or discarding something in its entirety when only part of it is unacceptable.

Don't wash your dirty linen in public

Do not discuss private disputes or family scandals in public.

Don't wish too hard; you might just get what you wished for

Beware of wishing for something too much, because you might not like it when you get it.

Don't bark if you can't bite

Don't complain if you can't enforce your point of view.

Don't count your chickens before they are hatched

Do not make plans based on something that has not happened.

Don't dig your grave with our own knife and fork

Don't do something that causes your own downfall.

Don't go near the water until you learn how to swim

Do not try to do something before you have learnt how to do it or before you are ready for it

Don't judge a book by its cover

Don't judge someone by their appearances.

Don't make a mountain out of a molehill

Do not make an issue over something small.

Don't mend what isn't broken

Do not change things that are working fine as they are.

Don't put all your eggs in one basket

One should not risk everything he has in a single venture.

Don't shut the barn door after the horse is gone

prepare for emergencies and eventualities before they happen

Don't teach your grandmother how to suck eggs

Do not be presumptuous and teach an experienced person how things should be done.

Dream of a funeral and you hear of a marriage

According to popular superstition, if you dream about a funeral you will shortly receive news that somebody of your acquaintance is to be married.

Drive gently over the stones

Take a cautious and delicate approach to any problems or difficulties you encounter in life.

E

Easier said than done
It is easier to say something than to actually do it.

East is East and West is West and never the twain shall meet
People who are very different in background or outlook are likely never to agree.

East or West, home is best
You feel safest, most comfortable and most at peace in your own home

Easy come, easy go
Things that are easily acquired, especially money, are just as easily lost or spent.

Eat to live, but do not live to eat
Man was created for a divine purpose and he has a destiny with his Creator - he was not born just to enjoy food.

Education doesn't come by bumping your head against the schoolhouse
Education can only be acquired by studying, and by listening and talking to teachers.

Elbow grease is the best polish
Hard work provides the best results.

Empty vessels make the most noise.
The least intelligent people are the most talkative.

Empty vessels make the most sound
Foolish people are the most talkative; often used as a put-down to somebody who chatters incessantly.

Enough is as good as a feast
A moderate amount is sufficient; often said by somebody who does not want any more.

Even a blind pig occasionally picks up an acorn
An incompetent person or an unsystematic approach is bound to succeed every now and then by chance.

Even a broken/stopped clock is right twice a day
Even a bad person has some amount of goodness.

Even a broken/stopped clock is right twice a day
No one is ever wrong all the time

Even a dog can distinguish between being stumbled over and being kicked
Do not let people bully you, but be alert to when you are being taken advantage of

Even a worm will turn
Even the most humble or submissive person will ultimately respond in anger to excessive harassment or exploitation.

Even Homer sometimes nods
Even the best of us are liable to make mistakes.

Every ass likes to hear himself bray
People like to listen to themselves talking.

Every ass loves to hear himself bray
Conceited people love to boast about their achievements

Every bird loves to listen to himself sing
People who know they are good at something tend to boast about their ability

Every bullet has its billet
In a life threatening situation, destiny decides who will die and who will survive.

Every cloud has a silver lining
if you say that every cloud has a silver lining, you mean that every sad or unpleasant situation has a positive side to it. If you talk about silver lining you are talking about something positive that comes out of a sad or unpleasant situation.

Every cloud has a silver lining
There is a positive aspect to every situation.

Every dog has its day
Everyone gets a period of success during their lifetime.

Every dog is allowed one bite
Somebody may be forgiven for a single misdemeanor, provided that it does not happen again

Every employee tends to rise to his level of incompetence
People in a hierarchical organization are promoted until they reach a position that is just beyond their capabilities; this cynical observation implies that nobody is fit to do the work he or she is employed to do.

Every family has a skeleton in the cupboard
Every family has their secrets

Every flow must have its ebb
Life has its ups and downs, neither good fortune nor ill fortune lasts forever.

Every herring must hang by its own gill
Everybody must take responsibility for his or her own actions.

Every horse thinks its own pack heaviest
Everybody thinks that he or she has harder work, greater misfortune, or more problems than others.

Every man after his fashion
Every individual must follow his or her own inclination.

Every man for himself and the devil take the hindmost
In highly competitive or dangerous situations, you must guard or pursue your own interests with ruthless disregard for those who are falling behind or struggling to cope.

Every man for himself
One should think of one's own interests before the interests of others.

Every man has his faults
No one is perfect

Every man has his price
If you offer someone enough money, he will be willing to do anything for you

Every man is his own worst enemy
A lot of people tend to hurt their own chance at success because

of negative-mindedness, fear, ignorance, unresolved issues

Every man is the architect of his own fortune

Life is what you make it.

Very man must carry his own cross

Everyone has to carry his burden or responsibilities in life

Every man must skin his own skunk

People should be self-reliant and not depend on others to do things—especially unpleasant tasks—for them.

Every man thinks his own geese swans

Everybody tends to rate his or her own children, possessions, or achievements more highly than others would do.

Every oak must be an acorn

Everything has to have a small beginning.

Every path has its puddle

The path of progress is always difficult.

Every picture tells a story

Meaning is often conveyed by people's actions, movements, gestures, or facial expressions without the need for words.

Every rose has its thorn

Every good thing has an unpleasant side.

Every soldier has the baton of a field marshal in his knapsack

A common soldier, or any other worker, may aspire to senior rank.

Every tub must stand on its own bottom

People should be self-sufficient and not dependent on others, financially or otherwise.

Every why has a wherefore

There is an explanation for everything.

Everybody has his fifteen minutes of fame

Most people will find themselves briefly in the public eye at least once in their lives.

Everybody talks about the weather, but nobody does anything about it

People are always ready to complain about a problem but never willing to solve it.

Everybody to whom much is given, of him will much be required

More is expected of those who have received more—that is, those who have had good fortune, are naturally gifted, or have been shown special favor.

Everybody's business is nobody's business

Matters that are of general concern, but are the responsibility of nobody in particular, tend to get neglected because everybody thinks that somebody else should deal with them.

Everybody's queer but you and me, and even you are a little queer

There are times when it seems that you are the only normal or sane person in the world.

Everyone can find fault, few can do better

It is easy to find faults in others, but difficult to correct oneself.

Everyone wants to go to heaven, but no one wants to die

Everyone wants to enjoy success, but few are willing to work hard or take the risks involved in achieving it

Everything in the garden is rosy

Everything is satisfactory.

Evil communications corrupt good manners

Good people can be led astray by listening to bad ideas, associating with bad people, or following a bad example.

Evil doers are evil dreaders

Criminals and other wrongdoers have a tendency to fear and suspect all those around them; sometimes used to imply that a distrustful person has something on his or her conscience.

Example is better than precept

It is better to show by example than to advise, order or tell people to be upright

Experience is the best teacher

The best way to learn something is to do it.

Experience is the father of wisdom

Experience and knowledge result in better judgement.

Experience is the mother of wisdom

You become wiser as you gain more experience in life

Experience is the teacher of fools

It is foolish to learn—or to expect other people to learn—solely by making mistakes; also used with the implication that wise people learn from others' mistakes rather than their own.

Extremes meet/opposites attract

People and things that seem to be diametrically opposed are often found to have a point of contact.

F

Fact is stranger than fiction

Things that happen in real life are often far more unlikely than those dreamed up by writers.

Facts are stubborn things

You cannot change the facts of a case

Facts speak louder than words

People show what they are really like by what they do, rather than by what they say.

Failure teaches success

Learning from one's mistakes will provide success in the future.

Faint heart never won fair lady

Be courageous if you want to achieve success.

Fair exchange is no robbery

Bartering two items that are of equal value is an honest deal.

Faith will move mountains

Miracles will happen when you believe that they will

Fall down seven times, stand up eight

One should keep trying so that even after many failures one succeeds someday.

False friends are worse than open enemies.

An enemy is better than a friend who stabs one behind one's back.

Familiarity breeds contempt

People tend to lose respect for people they are close to or in close company with all the time

Fancy passes beauty

It is more important that a potential partner is likeable than good-looking.

Fear is stronger than love

Fear is often a stronger emotion or motivation than even love

Fear lends wings

Fear inspires extra speed in those attempting to escape whatever threatens them.

Fear of death is worse than death itself

Fear is often a crippling emotion because it is so powerful

Feed a cold and starve a fever

You should eat well when you have a cold but fast when you have a fever.

Fields have eyes and woods have ears

There are very few places where you can do or say something without the risk of being seen or overheard.

Fine feathers make fine birds

You can pretend to be rich, famous etc. by dressing the part

Fine words butter no parsnips

Talking can't replace action. One should do rather than just say.

Fire is a good servant but a bad master

Fire has to be used wisely.

First catch your hare

Do not act in anticipation of something that is yet to be achieved.

First come, first served

The first person to arrive is attended to first.

First deserve, then desire

Before you begin to hope about possessing something, make sure you are qualified for it

First things first

Do important tasks first.

First think, and then speak

Think about what you are going to say before you speak

First try and then trust

Before relying upon something/one, it is best to test it first.

Fish or cut bait

The time has come to choose between two courses of action— either get on with what you have to do, or go away and let somebody else do it.

Flattery brings friends, truth enemies

People like to hear good things said about them although they may not be the truth

Flattery, like perfume, should be smelled but not swallowed

There is no harm in taking pleasure from flattery, but do not make the mistake of believing it.

Fling/throw mud at someone

To say evil or bad things about someone and in doing so, to damage his or her reputation.

Food without hospitality is medicine

It is hard to enjoy refreshments that are offered with ill grace, or without friendly companionship.

Fool me once, shame on you. fool me twice, shame on me

You should be alert to people trying to get the better of you

Fools and children should never see half done work

You should not judge the quality of a piece of work until it is complete, because it often appears unpromising in its unfinished form; sometimes said in response to criticism, or as a reason for not letting such work be seen.

Fools build houses and wise men live in them

The cost of building property is such that those who build houses cannot afford to live in them, and have to sell them to recoup their losses; also applied to other things that are expensive to produce

Fools rush in where angels fear to tread

Foolish people tend to act too hastily and do things that wise people would avoid.

Fools rush in where angels fear to tread.

Inexperienced people become involved in situations that more intelligent people avoid.

Footprints on the sands of time are not made by sitting down

People who idle their lives away will not make a lasting impression on history or be remembered for their great achievements; used as a spur to action and industry.

For want of a nail the shoe was lost, for want of a shoe the horse was lost, and for want of a horse the rider was lost

Do not neglect minor details that seem insignificant in themselves.

Forbidden fruit is sweet

Things that you must not have or do are always the most desirable.

Forewarned is forearmed

One can prepare for a risky situation by planning beforehand.

Forgive, but don't forget

Let go of situations but don't forget what they meant to you.

Fortune knocks once at every man's door

Everyone gets at least one good opportunity in his lifetime; everyone has the opportunity to be successful in life.

Four eyes see more than two

Two people keeping watch, supervising, or searching have a better chance of noticing or finding something.

Fretting cares make grey hairs

Worrying is a negative activity that can age you prematurely

Friendship is like money, easier made than kept

Effort is necessary to keep friendships alive.

From the sweetest wine, the tartest vinegar.

Great love may turn to the intense hatred; also used of other changes of feeling or nature from one extreme to the other.

From those to whom much is given, much is expected

Good results are expected from people to whom opportunities are awarded.

G

Garbage in, garbage out

A person or machine provided with inferior source material, faulty instructions, or erroneous information can produce only poor-quality work or rubbish.

Gardens are not made by sitting in the shade

Nothing is achieved without effort.

Gardens are not made by sitting in the shade

Nothing is achieved without any effort.

Gather ye rosebuds while ye may

Live life to the full while you are still young enough to enjoy it.

Genius is an infinite capacity for taking pains

What appears to be a product of superior intellectual power is often simply the result of great assiduity and meticulous attention to detail.

Give a beggar a horse and he'll ride it to death

People who suddenly acquire wealth or power are likely to misuse it.

Give a loaf and beg a slice

People who are too generous risk having to beg themselves.

Give a man a fish and you feed him for a day; teach a man to fish and you feed him for a lifetime

It is better to teach people how to be independent by teaching them how to do things for themselves than to do everything for them

Give a man an inch and he'll take a mile

People are inclined to take excessive advantage of the tolerance or generosity of others; often used to warn against making even the smallest concession.

Give a man enough rope and he'll hang himself

People who are given complete freedom of action will ultimately bring about their own downfall, for example by inadvertently revealing their guilt.

Give a thing, and take a thing, to wear the devil's gold ring

It is wrong to take back a gift.

Give and take is fair play

You should be willing to give in partly to others if you want them to give in partly to you

Give credit where credit is due

Appreciate someone for the good work he ahs done.

Give him an inch and he'll want a yard

Some people always take advantage of favor that is shown them

Give the devil his due

People deserve recognition for their skills and contributions even if they are otherwise unworthy or unlikable.

Go abroad and you'll hear news of home

People often remain ignorant of matters concerning their family and friends, or events in their own neighborhood,until they go traveling, when they hear about them at second hand.

Go farther and fare worse

If you reject something acceptable in the hope of finding something better, you may end up having to settle for something worse.

Go from the sublime to the ridiculous

To move from a wonderful situation to a bad one.

God helps those who help themselves.

Real effort ensures success.

God made the country and man made the town

The urban environment, constructed by human hands, is inferior to the natural countryside, which is the work of divine creation.

God never sends mouths but he sends meat

God can be relied upon to provide for everybody.

God sends meat, but the devil sends cooks

Good food can be ruined by a bad cook.

God tempers the wind to the shorn lamb

Weak or vulnerable people have divine protection from the worst misfortunes; also used when such people are treated with compassion by their fellow human beings.

Gold may be bought too dear

Wealth is not worth having if there is too great a risk or sacrifice involved in acquiring it.

Good accounting makes good friends

one will keep one's friends if one avoids disputes over money.

Good and quickly seldom meet

A well-done job takes time.

Good fences make good neighbors

A good relationship between neighbors depends on each respecting the other's privacy and not entering his or her property uninvited; also used more broadly of international relations and the need to maintain trade barriers and border controls.

Good management is better than good income

Income can be lost if it is used carelessly.

Good riddance to bad rubbish

We are better off without worthless people or things; usually said on the departure of such a person or the loss of such a thing.

Good wine needs no bush

Products of good quality do not need a lot of advertising, as their quality alone shows their worth

Goodness is better than beauty

Inner beauty is more valuable than outer beauty

Gossip is the lifeblood of society

Social intercourse thrives on gossip—if people stopped talking about each other they might stop talking to each other.

Grace will last, beauty will blast

A good character will outlive superficial physical attractiveness.

Grasp all, lose all

If you try to obtain everything you may risk losing everything you already have.

Great haste makes great waste

If one does things hastily he will make a lot of mistakes - he will need to spend a lot of time correcting those mistakes later.

Great men have great faults.

Remarkable people tend to have serious character flaws.

Great minds think alike

Wise people will normally think and behave alike in certain situations.

Great oaks grow from small acorns

Large successful operations can begin in a small way.

Great talkers are little doers

Those people who talk a lot and are always teaching others usually do not do much work.

Great trees keep down little ones

The predominance of a particular person, company, nation, etc., results in lesser rivals being kept in the shade.

Green leaves and brown leaves fall from the same tree

Everyone has a common beginning, and therefore, no one is above another

Grief divided is made lighter.

If you share your grief, it will be easier to bear.

Grin and bear it

To put up with discomfort or a bad situation without complaining.

H

Habit is second nature

An act done repeatedly and often enough will sooner or later become a habit or second nature.

Half a loaf is better than none

It's better to receive something than to receive nothing at all.

Half a loaf is better than none

You should be grateful for something, even if it is not as much as you wanted.

Half the truth is often a whole lie

Not telling the whole truth, or saying something that is only partly true, is tantamount to lying.

Handsome is what handsome does.

Behaviour is more important than appearance.

Hanging and wiving go by destiny

Some people are fated to marry each other, just as some are fated to be hanged.

Happy is the bride that the sun shines on

According to popular superstition, a woman who has a sunny wedding day will have a happy marriage.

Happy is the country that has no history

It is a happy or fortunate country that has no unpleasant events worth recording in its past.

Happy wife, happy life

If you have a happy or good life partner, you will be happy and contented

Hard cases make bad law

Cases that are complex or difficult to decide often cause the true meaning of the law to be distorted or obscured and sometimes lead to what is perceived as a miscarriage of justice.

Hard words break no bones

Ignore insults as they cannot physically harm you, and will only harm you emotionally if you let them.

Haste makes waste

Things that are done in a hurry are usually done sloppily, and may contain careless mistakes.

Hatred is as blind as love

A person who feels hatred does not see any qualities in the person he/she hates.

Hatred is as blind as love

A person who feels hatred does not see any qualities in the person he/she hates.

Have an old head on young shoulders

referring to mature youngsters who possess qualities that can be found only in older people.

Have eyes in the back of one's head
To know what is happening without seeing it.

Hawks will not pick out hawks' eyes
People who belong to the same group will not—or should not— harm one another.

He can who believes he can
If you believe you can do something, you will be able to do it.

He comes too early who brings bad news
People are never in a hurry to hear bad news.

He gives twice who gives quickly
A prompt response to a request for something, such as money or help, is of greater value than a more generous offering given late.

He has enough who is content
A happy person needs nothing more.

He is rich who owes nothing
A person who owes no one a debt is free of worry, and therefore, rich, in a sense

He is the best general who makes the fewest mistakes
A good leader rarely makes mistakes

He knows most who speaks last
The one who waits to listen to what others have to say before speaking has a better understanding of a situation

He laughs best who laughs last
Don't express your joy, or triumph, too soon.

He that complies against his will is of his own opinion still
By forcing somebody to do something, or to admit that something is true, you have not actually succeeded in changing that person's mind.

He that goes a-borrowing, goes a -sorrowing
Do not make borrowing a habit as you will suffer for it in the end

He that has a full purse never wanted a friend
Wealthy people never lack friends—or those who claim to be their friends until their money runs out.

He that is down need fear no fall
Those in lowly positions, or who have already fallen from lofty positions, have no need to worry about failure.

He that is master of himself, will soon be master of masters
Self-discipline will help you achieve greatness

He that is too secure is not safe
Beware of complacency—you must remain alert and watchful if you want to avoid danger.

He that knows nothing, doubts nothing
An ignorant person usually raises no questions because he is not aware that problems exist

He that lives in hope dances to an ill tune
It is unwise to let your future happiness or well-being depend on expectations that may not be realized.

He that lives on hope will die fasting
Do not pin all your hopes on something you may not attain, because you could end up with nothing.

He that plants thorns must never expect to gather roses

If you do evil, do not expect good to come to you

He that touches pitch shall be defiled

If you get involved with wicked people or illegal activities, you cannot avoid becoming corrupted yourself.

He that will not when he may, when he will he may have nay

Take advantage of an opportunity when it presents itself, even if you do not want or need it at the time, because it may no longer be available when you do.

He that will thrive must first ask his wife

A married man's financial situation, his success or failure in business, and the like often depend on the behavior and disposition of his wife.

He that would go to sea for pleasure would go to hell for a pastime

A sailor's life can be so unpleasant and dangerous, it seems that those who choose spend their leisure hours at sea must be either masochistic or insane.

He that would hang his dog gives out first that he is mad

Those who are planning some action that might attract criticism first seek to justify it in advance.

He that would have eggs must endure the cackling of hens

You must be prepared to put up with something unpleasant or annoying in order to get what you want; also used of an undesirable aspect or drawback that accompanies something.

He who dares, wins

You can only win or succeed if you are willing to take risks

He who fails to prepare, prepares to fail

Lack of preparation will cause you to lose or fail

He who fights and runs away may live to fight another day

It is wiser to withdraw from a situation that you cannot win than to go on fighting and lose—by a strategic retreat you can return to the battle or argument with renewed energy at a later date.

He who hesitates is lost

You will lose opportunities if you are indecisive and not fast enough to grab them

He who is everywhere is nowhere.

It's not good to do too many things at the same time.

He who knows does not speak. He who speaks does not know

It is an ironic situation when someone who should speak up does not while the person who should not, does

He who knows nothing doubts nothing

Knowledge leads us to make choices.

He who laughs last, laughs longest

Minor successes or failures along the way are of no significance—the person who is ultimately triumphant is the only real winner; often used when somebody turns the tables with a final act of retaliation.

He who likes borrowing dislikes paying

People who tend to borrow often are usually slow in settling debts

He who lives too fast, goes to his grave too soon

If you do not allow yourself to rest once in a while when you lead a fast-paced life, you will suffer from stress, burnt out and illness

He who pays the piper calls the tune

The person who pays for a service or finances a project has the right to say how it should be done.

He who plays with fire gets burnt

If you behave in a risky way, you are likely to have problems.

He who rides a tiger is afraid to dismount

When you are in a dangerous situation, or have embarked on a dangerous course of action, it is often safer to continue than to try to stop or withdraw.

He who serves two masters must lie to one

You cannot effectively or fully serve two people as your attention, loyalty, commitment etc. will be split between the two

He who sleeps forgets his hunger

Sleeping is a good way to forget you are hungry, especially when there is no food for you and you have no money to buy any.

He who stands for nothing will fall for everything

A person with no principles or opinions of his own will tend to go along with anything anyone tells him, and can, therefore, be easily cheated.

He who sups with the devil should have a long spoon

Those who have dealings with wicked, dangerous, or dishonest people should remain on their guard and try not to become too intimately involved.

He who will steal an egg will steal an ox

A person who steals small things is likely to steal big things too

He who wills the end wills the means

If you are determined to do something you will find a way.

He who wills the end wills the means

If you are determined to do something you will find a way.

He who would write and can't write can surely review

People who become critics are those who lack the talent to be novelists, dramatists, or other kinds of artists in their own right; used in response to a bad review.

Heads I win, tails you lose

In some situations it is impossible for one person not to be a winner—or impossible for another person not to be a loser—whatever the outcome.

Health is better than wealth

It's better to be in good health than to be rich.

Hear all, see all, say nowt

It is sometimes prudent to listen and watch carefully, but say nothing.

Hell hath no fury like a woman scorned

A woman who is rejected by the man she loves has an immense capacity for ferocious or malicious revenge.

Help you to salt, help you to sorrow
According to popular superstition, it is unlucky to add salt to another person's food at table.

Hide your light under a bushel
Concealing your talents, skills or abilities

History is a fable agreed upon
History represents the traditionally accepted interpretation of what actually happened in the past.

History repeats itself
Similar events tend to recur in different periods of history— for example, when rulers or governments fail to learn from the mistakes of those who have gone before; also used when some more trivial or personal incident recurs; What has happened once is liable to happen again.

Hitch one's wagon to a star
To move forward in a way to improve your chances of achieving success.

Home is home, be it ever so homely
However simple or lowly a person's abode may be, it is still his or her home and therefore the best place to be.

Home is where the heart is
You call home the place where the people you love are.

Homer sometimes nods
Even the greatest minds have lapses of attention, leading to mistakes; often used as an excuse for error.

Honest men marry quickly, wise men not at all
Honest men marry without hesitation, seeing no threat in a wife, but wise men know better.

Honesty is the best policy
It's always better to be honest.

Honey catches more flies than vinegar
You can obtain more cooperation from others by being nice.

Honors change manners
People who improve their status in society all too often become arrogant.

Hope for the best, expect the worst
Never lose hope, but be prepared with an alternative if things do not go as planned

Hope is a good breakfast but a bad supper
There is no harm in being optimistic at the beginning of something, but beware of being left with nothing but unrealized expectations at the end.

Hope is life
To live is to always be hopeful

Hope is the last thing that we lose
People are by nature hopeful, and must always be so because when we lose hope, we lose the will to live

Hope springs eternal in the human breast
It is human nature to remain optimistic— even after a setback, or despite evidence to the contrary.

Hope springs eternal
Hope is something that never dies, and people should never lose hope.

Horses for courses
Different people have different strengths and talents, and each person should be assigned to the task or job that is best suited to that particular individual.

However long the night, the dawn will break.
Bad things don't last forever.

However long the night, the dawn will break.
Bad things don't last forever.

Humble hearts have humble desires.
People with timid characters tend to have modest ambitions.

Hunger drives the wolf out of the wood
People in dire need are forced to do things that would be unwise or undesirable in other circumstances.

Hunger is a good sauce
All food tastes good when you are hungry.

Hunger is the best sauce
Hunger makes all food taste good, regardless of its quality or the way it is served.

Hunger is the best spice
When you are really hungry, everything tastes good, and you eat up everything placed in front of you

Hurry no man's cattle
Do not try to make others hurry or rush because you are impatient.

I

If a camel gets his nose in a tent, his body will follow
If you let something intrusive enter your life, your life will become difficult.

If a camel gets his nose in a tent, his body will follow
If you let something intrusive enter your life, your life will become difficult.

If and an spoils many a good charter
Excellent plans may be doomed to failure because of the conditions that come with them.

If at first you don't succeed, try, try again
Never stop trying to succeed at something

If in February there be no rain, 'tis neither good for hay nor grain
Plants and grains will grow badly if there is no rain in early spring.

If it looks like a duck, walks like a duck, and quacks like a duck, it's a duck
It is usually safe to identify somebody as a particular type of person when his or her appearance, behavior, and words all point to the same conclusion.

If it's not one thing it's another
Troubles seem never ending.

If one sheep leaps over the ditch, all the rest will follow
Where one person sets an example by doing something risky or dangerous others are likely to follow.

If the blind lead the blind, both shall fall into the ditch
Those without knowledge should not try to teach the ignorant.

If the shoe fits, wear it
If something said about you is true, you should accept it.

If the sky falls, we shall catch larks
Do not make plans based on things that cannot possibly happen.

If two ride a horse, one must ride behind.
When two people do something together, one will be the leader and the other will be the subordinate.

If two ride a horse, one must ride behind
When two prople do something together, one will be the leader and the other will be the subordinate; also used of a fight argument, where only one can win and the other must lose or surrender.

If wishes were horses, beggars would ride

There is no point in indulging in wishful thinking.

If you are patient in one moment of anger, you will avoid 100 days of sorrow

Avoid regrets by taking the time to think before speaking or acting angrily.

If you buy cheaply, you pay dearly

Cheap goods are usually not the best in terms of quality

If you buy quality, you only cry once

Items of good quality may be expensive, but they will last you a long time

If you can't bite, never show your teeth

Do not make empty threats; also used to warn against making a show of aggression when you unable to defend yourself.

If you can't run with the big dogs, stay under the porch

If you lack the strength, courage, skill, or experience to compete with the major players—in politics, business, or any other field—then it is better not to try at all.

If you can't lick them, join them

If you cannot defeat an opponent or get him to change his ideas, plans or way of doing things, the best thing is to change your ideas, plans, etc.

If you can't take the heat, get out of the kitchen

If you cannot handle something, give it up

If you chase two rabbits, you will not catch either one

If you try to do two things at the same time, you will not succeed in doing either of them.

If you don't like it, you can lump it

Whether or not you like what is offered or approve of what is proposed, you will have to put up with it.

If you don't buy a ticket, you can't win the raffle

If you do not take the risk, you cannot expect success

If you don't have anything nice to say, don't say anything at all

Avoid being negative

If you keep your mouth shut, you won't put your foot in it

Keep quiet, and you will say nothing wrong

If you pay peanuts, you get monkeys

Competent and highly qualified people will not work for derisory fees or wages.

If you want a friend, be a friend

Friendship must be reciprocal.

If you want a thing done right, do it yourself

Do not rely on others to complete your work for you.

If you want peace, prepare for war

A nation that is seen to be ready and able to defend itself—for example, with strong armed forces and powerful weapons—is less likely to be attacked.

If you were born to be shot, you'll never be hanged

You cannot escape your fate

If you've got it, flaunt it

Those who have wealth, beauty,

or talent should not be ashamed to show it off; used as an excuse for ostentation.

If you're in a hole, stop digging

Do not create more trouble for yourself when you are already facing some

Ignorance is a voluntary misfortune

Everybody has the opportunity to acquire knowledge, so you have only yourself to blame if you remain ignorant.

Ignorance is bliss

You can be happy when you do not know there are problems around you

Ignorance of the law excuses no man

Not knowing what you did was wrong does not excuse you from suffering the penalty.

Ill weeds grow apace

Worthless people or evil things have a tendency to flourish where better ones fail.

Imitation is the sincerest form of flattery

When someone copies what you do, it means they really admire you or the way you do things.

In for a penny, in for a pound

Once you have committed yourself to something, you might as well do it wholeheartedly and see it through to the end.

In politics a man must learn to rise above principle

A successful politician cannot afford to have too many scruples; a cynical observation.

In the land of the blind the one-eyed man is king

A man of limited ability has an advantage over a person who is less able.

In the mind of thieves the moon is always shining

Criminal minds are always cautious about getting caught.

In times of prosperity friends are plentiful

You have many friends when you have no difficulties.

In times of prosperity friends are plentiful

You have many friends when you have no difficulties.

In war there is no substitute for victory

A war is only truly won by total defeat of the enemy, not by diplomatic negotiations or compromise.

It is always darkest before the dawn

The most difficult time is just before the problem is solved.

It is best to be on the safe side

Play safe, and be prepared for the worst to happen

It is useless to flog a dead horse

It is no use spending your time and energy on an activity or belief that is already widely rejected or outdated.

It never rains but it pours

One setback, misfortune, or other undesirable occurrence is inevitably followed by many more; also occasionally used of pleasant things, such as a run of good luck.

It takes a village to raise a child

The whole community plays a part in the upbringing of the children that live there.

It takes all sorts to make a world

People vary in character and abilities, and this is a good thing.

It takes one to know one

Only those with similar flaws are capable of spotting them in others.

It takes two to make a quarrel

Both parties in a quarrel should share the blame or take responsibility for it; no one can start a quarrel all by himself.

It takes two to tango

In a situation involving cooperation or joint action, both participants must work together and share the responsibility for what happens.

It's a foolish sheep that makes the wolf his confessor

Do not confide in somebody unless you are certain that he or she can be trusted.

It's a poor dog that's not worth whistling for

Everybody has some value, or some redeeming feature.

It's all in a day's work

Unpleasant things have to be accepted as part of the daily routine; also used to play down a major achievement or a heroic act by implying that it is just part of your job.

It's an ill bird that fouls its own nest

You should not say or do anything that will bring discredit or harm to your own family or country.

It's better to be happy than wise

Happiness is more important than wisdom, knowledge, or learning.

It's better to be right than in the majority

Do not follow or side with the majority just for the sake of conformity, if you believe them to be wrong.

It's better to lose the battle than win the war

It is sometimes prudent or expedient to concede a minor point in an argument or dispute in order to gain the overall victory.

It's dogged as does it

Anything can be done with determination and perseverance.

It's easy to find a stick to beat a dog.

It is easy to find some reason or excuse to justify a critical attack or a harsh punishment.

It's good to make a bridge of gold to a flying enemy

Retreating enemies will kill or destroy anybody or anything that stands in their way, so it is advisable to give them free passage.

It's idle to swallow the cow and choke on the tail

Once you have completed the major part of an enterprise or undertaking, it is foolish not to see it through to the end.

It's ill jesting with edged tools

Do not trifle with dangerous things or people.

It's ill sitting at Rome and striving with the Pope

It is foolish or pointless to quarrel or fight with somebody who has supreme power in the place where you are.

It's ill speaking between a full man and a fasting

Hungry people are not on the best of terms with those who have eaten their fill.

It's ill waiting for dead men's shoes

It is not good to be impatiently awaiting somebody's death or retirement to get what you want, such as an inheritance or promotion.

It's not the end of the world

Things are not as disastrous as they seem; said in recurrence, such as after a minor mishap.

It's the last straw that breaks the camel's back

When somebody is close to his or her limit of patience or endurance, it takes only one little extra thing to make the whole load too much to bear.

It's a blessing in disguise

When an opportunity arrives through a crisis etc.

It's an ill wind that blows nobody any good

A bad or evil occurrence.

It's better to give than to receive

Giving is more blessed than receiving

It's better to have loved and lost than never to have loved at all

Do not be afraid to fall in love

It's never too late to mend

It is never too late to correct one's mistakes or faults.

It's no use crying over spilt milk

Don't express regret for something that has happened and cannot be remedied.

J

Jack of all trades and master of none

Is a person who can do almost anything, but he rarely excels in any of them.

Jack's as good as his master

everybody may be equal but some people (or animals) are more equal than others.

Jam tomorrow and jam yesterday, but never jam today

Good times always seem to belong to the past or to the future, but never to the present.

Jesters do oft prove prophets.

A prediction made in jest often comes true.

Jove but laughs at lovers' perjury

The breaking of oaths and promises made by lovers is so commonplace that it is not regarded as a serious matter.

Judge not, lest ye be judged

Do not judge others as you are not perfect yourself, so be merciful in the hope that others will show you mercy one day

Jump from the frying pan into the fire

To go from bad to worse.

Justice delayed is justice denied

If the law is applied too late, there is no justice.

Justice delayed is justice denied.

If the law is applied too late, there is no justice.

Justice is blind

Justice must be dispensed with objectivity and without regard to irrelevant details or circumstances.

Justice pleased few in their own house

One does not blame oneself for anything.

K

Keep a thing seven years and you'll find a use for it

An object that seems useless now may be just what you need at some future time, so do not discard it.

Keep no more cats than will catch mice

Do not acquire more than what you need

Keep the wolf from the door

To avoid hunger and poverty

Keep your eyes wide open before marriage, half shut afterward

You should choose your husband or wife with care, but be prepared to overlook his or her faults after the wedding day.

Keep your friends close, and your enemies closer

Keep track of what your enemies are up to for your own protection

Keep your mouth shut & your eyes open.

Talk less and work more.

Kill not the goose that laid the golden egg

Do not be so foolish as to destroy the source of your good fortune out of pride, greed, anger etc.

Kill one to warn a hundred

Warn many by punishing a few.

Kill two birds with one stone

Complete two tasks with one action

Kindle not a fire you cannot put out

Do not start something you cannot control or resolve

Kindle not a fire you cannot put out

Do not start something that you cannot control; you may fail or cause damage.

Kindness begets kindness

When you are kind to people, they will be kind to you in return

Kings have long arms

Few people, places, or things are beyond the reach of those in authority, and it is not easy for an offender to escape capture or punishment.

Kissing goes by favor

People often bestow honors and privileges on those they like, rather than on those who are most worthy of them.

Knowledge and timber shouldn't be much used until they are seasoned

Knowledge is not useful until it is tempered by experience.

Knowledge in youth is wisdom in age

What you learn when you are young will be invaluable when you grow old.

Knowledge in youth is wisdom in age

What you learn when you are young will be invaluable when your grow old.

Knowledge is power

The more you learn, the greater influence you have over others.

L

Late children, early orphans
Children to older parents run a greater risk of being orphaned before they reach adulthood

Laugh and grow fat
Laughter creates a sense of well-being and happiness

Laugh and the world laughs with you
When someone is in a happy, cheerful mood, people like being with him.

Laughter is the best medicine
being cheerful is good for your total well-being

Laughter is the shortest distance between two people
Laughter is the best way to break the ice between strangers or enemies

Learn to walk before you run.
Don't rush into doing something before you know how to do it.

Learning is a treasure that will follow its owner everywhere
Education is something that you keep forever.

Least said, soonest mended/forgotten
The less you say, the less likely you are to cause trouble; often used to discourage somebody from complaining, apologizing, arguing, or making excuses.

Leave well enough alone
Do not try to change or improve something that is satisfactory as it stands.

Lend your money and lose your friend
You risk losing your friends by lending them money, either because they fail to repay the loan or because they resent being asked to repay it.

Length begets loathing
Nobody likes a long-winded speaker or writer.

Less is more
A work of art, piece of writing, or other creative endeavor can be made more elegant or effective by reducing ornamentation and avoiding excess.

Let bygones be bygones
One should consider forgiving one's and forget all the bad deeds done by others.

Let him who is without sin cast the first stone
You qualify to judge someone only if you yourself are faultless.

Let sleeping dogs lie
One should preferably avoid discussing issues that are likely to create trouble.

Let the buyer beware
Always be aware of what you are getting yourself into.

Let the chips fall where they may.
Do not try to control your destiny.

Let the cobbler stick to his last
People should not offer advice, make criticisms, or otherwise interfere in matters outside their own area of knowledge or expertise.

Let the dead bury the dead
Do not concern yourself with things that are past and gone.

Let them laugh that win
Do not rejoice until you are certain of victory or success.

Let us go hand in hand, not one before another
Face problems together in unity, and not alone or in a spirit of enmity

Let your head save your heels
You can avoid wasted journeys on foot by careful planning or forethought, such as by combining errands.

Liars need good memories
People who lie should be careful to remember what they say.

Liberty is not licence
Freedom does not mean that a person can whatever he or she wants.

Life begins at forty
By this age, people gain a lot of experience and do not have a lot of responsibilities so they can easily enjoy life.

Life is hard by the yard, but by the inch life's a cinch
Life is less overwhelming if you take it one step at a time.

Life is just a bowl of cherries
Life is full of happiness and pleasure

Light gains make heavy purses
It is possible to become rich by making small profits.

Lightning never strikes twice in the same place
The same unpleasant or unexpected phenomenon will not recur in the same place or circumstances, or happen to the same person again; a superstition that often leads to a false sense of security.

Like cures like
People who have been through something are usually able to help others with the same problem

Like father, like son
A son can be expected to resemble his father in many ways.

Like people, like priest
The quality of a spiritual leader can be judged by the behavior of his or her followers.

Listeners never hear any good of themselves
People who eavesdrop on the conversations of others risk hearing unfavorable comments about themselves; used as a warning or reprimand.

Little birds that can sing and won't sing must be made to sing
Those who refuse to tell what they know must be forced to do so; also interpreted more literally.

Little boys should be seen and not heard
Children should not interrupt when adults are talking.

Little by little and bit by bit
If you persevere at something, you will gradually accomplish it.

Little enemies and little wounds must not be despised

Do not ignore people you have angered or hurt, however small the slight or injury, as they can harm you one day if they choose to bear a grudge

Little fish are sweet

The smallest things are sometimes the most desirable or acceptable; used specifically of something received, bought, or otherwise acquired.

Little pitchers have big ears

Children miss little of what is said in their hearing; often used as a warning.

Little strokes feel great oaks

Continuous effort, however small the mount, will help you achieve your greatest dreams and ambitions

Little strokes fell good oaks

Dividing a task into parts makes it easier to do.

Little thieves are hanged, but great ones escape

It is often the case that petty criminals are brought to justice, while those involved in more serious crimes succeed in evading capture and punishment.

Little things please little minds.

Foolish people are easily pleased; said contemptuously to or of somebody who is amused by something childish or trivial.

Live and learn

Learn as much as you can from life

Live and let live

Get on with your own affairs and let other get on with theirs.

Lock the stable door after the horse has bolted

Once a mistake has been made or an error committed, it's too late to take precautions to prevent it from happening.

Long absent, soon forgotten

If you are away for too long, people may forget you

Long foretold, long last; short notice, soon past

A change in the weather that is predicted well in advance lasts longer than one that arrives with little warning.

Look after the pence, and the pounds will look after themselves

Take care of the details and the bigger issues will be solved

Look at the bright side

Be optimistic

Look before you leap.

Consider possible consequences before taking action.

Look on the bright side

Be positive

Look on the sunny side of life

Be positive in life

Lookers-on see most of the game.

An objective observer with an overall view of a situation is often more knowledgeable, or better placed to make a judgment, than somebody who is actively involved, and whose attention is therefore focused on individual details.

Loose lips sink ships

People who talk too much may give away important secrets that could harm themselves or others.

Lose an hour in the morning, chase it all day

Time lost in the morning is impossible to make up later in the day.

Losers weepers, finders keepers

If someone loses something, he weeps – but if someone finds it, he keeps it.

Losers weepers, finders keepers.

If you lose something you lament, if you find something you keep it.

Love conquers all

Love motivates people to make things work

Love covers a multitude of sins

When you treat people with love, compassion, kindness, forebearing etc. you make up for a lot of your own faults because it is right to love people

Love is blind

A person in love does not see the faults of the person he/she loves.

Love is free

People tend to fall in love regardless of the suitability of the match or other obstacles.

Love laughs at locksmiths.

Nothing and nobody can keep lovers apart.

Love makes the world go round

Love is the important thing in life that makes life meaningful

Love me little, love me long

Warm affection lasts longer than burning passion.

Love me, love my dog

If you love somebody, you must be prepared to accept or tolerate everything and everybody connected with that person—his or her failings, idiosyncrasies, friends, relatives, and so on.

Love sees no faults

Real love does not take into account the flaws of a person

Love will find a way

Love motivates people to look for solutions to all problems

Love your enemy, but don't put a gun in his hand

Treat your enemies with respect and humanity, but also with caution— do not give them the opportunity to repay your kindness with an act of aggression.

M

Make a silk purse out of a sow's ear
Manage to product something good using poor material.

Make a virtue of necessity
The best way to handle an undesirable situation is to turn it to your advantage.

Make haste slowly
Do not rush—you will achieve your end more quickly if you proceed with care.

Make hay while the sun shines
Seize opportunities

Man cannot live by bread alone
It takes more than food to complete your life

Man is the head of the family and woman is the neck that turns the head
No comment!

Man is the measure of all things
Human beings are capable of rising to any challenge.

Man proposes, God disposes.
One's destiny depends on God's will.

Manners make the man
One's manners show one's character.

Many a true word is spoken in jest
Something said jokingly often proves to be true.

Many are called, but few are chosen
Not everybody who wants to do something is selected or permitted to do it; used in any elitist situation.

Many go out for wool and come home shorn
Many people who set out to make their fortune, or to achieve some other aim, end up in a worse state than before.

Many hands make light work
Sharing work makes the task easier.

Many kiss the hand they wish to see cut off
A person's true feelings or intentions may be concealed by the mask of politeness or hypocrisy; used to warn against being deceived by such a show.

March comes in like a lion and goes out like a lamb
Meaning that the weather at the beginning of March is stormy and is mild at the end of the month.

March winds and April showers bring forth May flowers

The storms and rain in March and April bring flowers in May.

Mark, learn and inwardly digest.

Note and reflect upon something in order to thoroughly assimilate it.

Marriage is a lottery

Whether a marriage succeeds or fails is all a matter of luck; also applied to the choice of a marriage partner.

Marry in haste, repent at leisure

Do not rush into marriage because if you marry the wrong person, you will spend the rest of your life regretting it

May chickens come cheeping

signifies that children who are born in the month of May are weak and delicate.

Measure twice, cut once

Consider your options carefully in order to make a good decision

Memory is the treasure of the mind.

A good memory is very precious.

Men are from Mars, women are from Venus

Men and women have different characteristics.

Men make houses, women make homes.

A man builds a house but it is a woman who makes it a home by loving and nurturing it and its members.

Might as well be hanged for a sheep as (for) a lamb

If the penalty is going to be same, you might as well commit the greater offence.

Mirrors do everything we do, but they cannot think for themselves

man-made devices have their limits, and cannot do everything humans can

Misery loves company

When people are sad they often like others to feel sad too.

Misery makes strange bedfellows

Sadness leads people to befriend strange people.

Money begets money

Having money allows one to make more money.

Money burns a hole in the pocket

People tend to waste money if they have a lot of it.

Money cannot buy happiness

You cannot buy joy, peace, contentment etc

Money doesn't grow on trees

You should not waste money because it is not plentiful or obtained easily.

Money has no smell

Money that comes from questionable sources is no different from—and no less acceptable than—money that comes from anywhere else

Money is the root of all evil

Money can lead people to commit crimes.

Money isn't everything

Riches cannot solve all your problems or bring you joy, peace, contentment etc.

Money makes the mare go

Money enables things to be done, and things are done faster or more readily for those who are willing and able to pay well

Money makes the world go round

People work hard and go through a lot of pain just to earn more money as if it is what keeps them going.

Money talks

Wealthy people have great influence.

Monkey see, monkey do

People without minds of their own tend to blindly do and say what others do and say

More die of food than famine

Excessive indulgence in the wrong type of food is a bigger killer than famine

More haste, less speed

The more you hurry, the slower you seem to progress because hurrying causes you to make mistakes

Much cry and little wool

Those who make the most noise, the loudest boasts, or the greatest promises often have the least to offer, are the least productive, or simply fail to deliver the goods

Much water goes by the mill that

The miller knows not of Many things are stolen or go astray without the knowledge of the person affected

Much would have more

People are never satisfied with what they have

N

Nature abhors a vacuum

There are no deficiencies in nature—whenever a gap or vacancy occurs, something or somebody will come along to fill it

Nature passes nurture

A person's inborn character, or inherited characteristics, cannot be changed by his or her upbringing.

Nature will have its course

There is no denying natural processes or impulses.

Nature, time and patience are three great physicians

The goodness of nature, time and being patient can bring healing

Ne'er cast a clout till

May be out Do not stop wearing any item of warm winter clothing before the end of May

Near is my shirt, but nearer is my skin

A person's own best interests take precedence over those of his or her friends and family

Necessity is the mother of invention

The need for something compels people to search for a method of obtaining it.

Necessity sharpens industry

Need makes people work harder

Need makes the old wife trot

Necessity provides a sense of urgency

Need teaches a plan

Necessity will make you find a solution.

Needs must when the devil drives

There are times when people are forced to do things that they would not do under normal circumstances

Needs must when the devil drives.

Sometimes you are compelled to do something that you would rather not do.

Neglect will kill an injury sooner than revenge

Insults and other malicious acts are forgotten most quickly when the victim chooses to ignore them

Never ask pardon before you are accused

If nobody knows that you have done something wrong, do not apologize and reveal your guilt— you may get away with it

Never choose your women or linen by candlelight

Soft or inadequate lighting can give people and things a deceptively attractive appearance, or hide their faults and flaws.

Never do evil that good may come of it

A wicked or immoral course of action cannot be vindicated by a worthy objective

Never do things by halves

One should not do an incomplete or imperfect job - certain tasks must not be left half done; they must be done away with immediately.

Never fall out with your bread and butter

Do not quarrel with the people who pay you your salary or with your customers.

Never give a sucker an even break

Foolish or gullible people are easily exploited and do not deserve a fair chance; used to justify taking advantage of such a person.

Never give advice unless asked

Do not assume that people need your help or that you have all the answers to help them, it is better to wait until you are asked for help.

Never is a long time

Think carefully before you use the word never, which implies a

certainty about the future that you cannot possess.

Never let the right hand know what the left hand is doing

Be discreet in all you do, do not tell others your deeds, especially your good deeds.

Never let the sun go down on your anger

If you have quarrelled or lost your temper with somebody, make your peace before the end of the day.

Never let your education interfere with your intelligence

There are times when never do evil that good may come of it you must trust your intuition or native wit rather than what you have been taught or what you have read

Never look a gift horse in the mouth

When you are offered something for nothing, accept it with gratitude and do not find fault with it.

Never marry for money, but marry where money is

It is good to marry somebody with sufficient means for a comfortable life,but wealth should not be your sole criterion in choosing a marriage partner

Never put off till tomorrow what you can do today

Do not delay doing tasks and assignments

Never say die

Do not surrender, stop trying, or give up hope

Never say never

Always leave room for change

Never send a boy to do a man's job

Do not assign a difficult task to somebody who lacks the strength, experience, or qualifications to do it properly; also used of inanimate objects, such as an inadequate piece of equipment or a low card that fails to win a trick.

Never speak ill of the dead

Do not talk badly about the departed.

Never speak of rope in the house of a man who has been hanged

Be tactful and steer clear of sensitive subjects in the company of people who might be upset or offended by them

Never tell tales out of school

Do not pass on confidential information, secrets, or gossip to others, especially to outsiders

Never trouble trouble till trouble troubles you

Do not go looking for trouble

Never work with children or animals

The unpredictability of children and animals make them unreliable as fellow-workers

New lords, new laws

When a new ruler or government comes to power—or when a new person takes control of a situation—changes are made and different rules apply

Night brings counsel

If you have a difficult problem to solve or an important decision to make, a good night's sleep will work wonders

Nine tailors make a man

A well-dressed person does not buy all his or her clothes from the same source

No good deed goes unpunished

When you do something kind or helpful you often get something unpleasant in return; a cynical observation

No joy without annoy

There is no happiness without some sadness.

No losers, no winners

If there are no losers, there are also no winners.

No man can serve two masters

You can only be faithful to one boss, leader etc.

No man is a hero to his valet

The better you know somebody, with all his or her faults and weaknesses, the less likely you are to regard that person with awe or veneration.

No man is a hero to his valet

There are few people who are admired by their peers who know them well.

No man is an island

Nobody can function in total isolation from the rest of society.

No man is content with his lot

Most people seem to be dissatisfied with what they have, and want other things.

No man is indispensable

No man is so useful to others that people cannot do without him.

No money, no justice

In a corrupt legal system, you can bribe lawyers and judges to win a case for you.

No names, no pack-drill

If no names are mentioned, nobody can be punished or held responsible for something.

No news is good news

When there is no news, it is likely that everything is all right.

No pain, no gain

You must be ready to make sacrifices to get what you want badly.

No rain, no grain

Without rain harvests will be poor.

No revenge is more honorable than the one not taken lips sink ships

However tempted you may be to retaliate, try not to because revenge is a negative pursuit.

No rose is without a thorn

Nothing on earth is perfect.

No smoke without fire

Rumours could contain some amount of truth.

No time like the present

Now is the best time to do something

Nobody is indispensable

Nobody is so important or well qualified that he or she cannot be replaced by another.

Nobody is perfect

Everybody makes mistakes.

None but the brave deserve the fair

Those who lack boldness or courage do not deserve to achieve great things;also used more literally, of men courting women—or vice versa

Nothing comes free

Unfortunately, everything in life has a price attached to it

Nothing is certain but the unforeseen

The one thing that is sure to happen is the thing that nobody expects or is prepared for; also used to imply that nothing can be predicted

Nothing should be done in haste but gripping a flea

There are very few things that need to be done quickly; said by somebody urged to hurry up

Nothing so bad but it might have been worse

Try to take a positive view of misfortune—things are never as bad as they could be

Nothing so bold as a blind mare

Those who are ignorant or unaware of danger proceed without fear or caution

Nothing succeeds like success

Successful people go on to ever

greater things; also used to imply that people are more respected or accepted after they succeed

Nothing succeeds like success

When a person starts being successful, he is likely to continue being successful

Nothing ventured nothing gained.

You cannot achieve anything without taking risks

Nothing ventured, nothing gained

You will not achieve anything unless you are prepared to make an attempt or take a risk

Nothing ventured, nothing gained

One must take risks in order to succeed at anything

Nought is never in danger

Persons or things of no value are at no risk of being stolen

O

Obey orders, if you break owners
Do as you are commanded, even if this means doing something you know to be foolish or wrong

Oil and water do not mix
Some people or things are incompatible by nature

Old habits die hard
It is difficult to change a long-time habit

Old sins cast long shadows
The passage of time often has the effect of making past wrongdoing seem greater or more significant than it actually was

Old soldiers never die
Those who have served in the armed forces and survived warfare often live so long that they seem indestructible

Once a priest, always a priest
People cannot change their vocation; also used to imply that people continue to behave in accordance with the habits and training of their trade or profession even after they have left it.

Once bitten twice shy
If a person has been tricked once he will more be careful and alert the next time.

One cannot love and be wise
People often show a lack of common sense or good judgment when they are in love.

One courageous thought will put to flight a host of troubles
A strong and positive mental attitude is the best defense against anxiety or adversity.

One enemy is too much
Having even a single enemy in the world is dangerous.

One father is (worth) more than a hundred schoolmasters.
A father matters more than a teacher.

One funeral makes many
Standing around a grave on a cold or rainy day is not good for the health, and can prove fatal for those attending a funeral.

One good turn deserves another
Always be ready to show kindness to people who have been kind to you.

One good turn deserves another.
Help someone who helps you.

One half of the world doesn't know how the other half lives
People have no conception or understanding of the problems

and pleasures of everyday life for those in other social classes, occupations, or countries; chiefly used of the contrast between rich and poor.

One hand for yourself and one for the ship

Do not neglect your own safety, security, or well-being for the sake of your work or your employers; also used literally as a safety maxim for those working at sea.

One hand washes the other

People cooperate and help one another, and expect favors to be reciprocated.

One hour's sleep before midnight is worth two after

Those who go to bed early have a more refreshing night's sleep than those who rise late in the morning.

One law for the rich and another for the poor

It sometimes seems that rich people are treated more leniently by the legal system than poor people

One man's loss is another man's gain

People profit from the misfortunes of others; also used more literally

One man's meat is another man's poison

What one person likes, another person dislikes

One man's trash is another man's treasure

Many people prize things that others would not give houseroom to.

One man's terrorist is another man's freedom fighter

There are always two sides to an argument and two perspectives to consider

One man's trash is another man's treasure

What is useless to one person could be precious to another.

One nail drives out another

One thing replaces another, or new ideas or customs cause old ones to fall into disuse.

One of these days is none of these days

Somebody who says he or she will do something "one of these days"—that is, at some unspecified future time—will probably never do it; said in response to such a person.

One picture is worth ten thousand words

Visual images are often the most concise and effective means of expression.

One story is good till another is told

People are happy to accept one idea until a new idea comes along to replace it.

One swallow doesn't make a summer

One success doesn't guarantee life-long success.

One sword keeps another in its scabbard

Showing that you are ready and able to defend yourself is a good way of discouraging others from attacking you.

One thief robs another

People who are dishonest will not scruple to steal from each other.

One today is worth two tomorrows.

What one has today is far better than what one hoped for.

One year's seeding makes seven years' weeding

If you allow weeds to seed themselves, it will take a long time to get rid of all the new plants they produce; also used figuratively of the need to eradicate something undesirable before it has a chance to spread, or to warn people that their actions can have lasting repercussions:

Only real friends will tell you when your face is dirty

Only a real friend tells one the truth.

Opportunities look for you when you are worth finding

Those who have good fortune are often those who best deserve it.

Opportunity seldom knocks twice.

Don't let go of opportunities. They are difficult to come.

Other times, other manners

Customs and conventions change over the years,and we should not judge people or things of the past by modern standards, or vice versa; sometimes said to those who mock or criticize the behavior of members of a different generation

Out of sight, out of mind

Friends with whom one is not in contact are soon forgotten.

Out of the fullness of the heart the mouth speaks

People cannot avoid talking about what is on their mind; also used to imply that a person's true thoughts and feelings are revealed by what he or she says

Out of the mouth of babes and sucklings

Children often speak sensibly.

P

Paper bleeds little

It is easy to do something in writing, without taking account of the human factors involved.

Paper does not blush

It is possible to express in writing what you would be too ashamed or embarrassed to say.

Parents are patterns

Parents are role models for their children and should set a good example.

Past cure, past care

It is futile worrying about something when it is too late to do anything about it.

Patience is a virtue

Patience is an advantage and a good trait to nurture in yourself.

Patriotism is the last refuge of a scoundrel

Those who have no better argument resort to appeals to patriotic sentiment.

Pay as you go and nothing you'll owe

It is best to pay for everything when you receive it and not to get into debt.

Pay beforehand was never well served

People who are paid in advance for their services have little incentive to work hard or well.

Peace makes plenty

Peace brings prosperity.

Penny wise, pound foolish

Referring to people who spend small amounts of money wisely but are equally foolish when it comes to spending big amounts of money.

People are more easily led than driven

It is better to guide people by example than to force them to do as they are told.

People who live in glass houses should not throw stones

Do not criticize others for their faults which may be similar to your own.

Physician, heal thyself

Do not reproach another person for something that you are equally guilty of; also used to imply that you should solve your own problems before you try to deal with those of other people.

Pigs are pigs

All bad people or things are equally undesirable, regardless of where they come from.

Pity is akin to love

Pity and love are related emotions.

Please your eye and plague your heart

Those who choose their husbands, wives, or lovers on the basis of good looks alone may suffer for their choice.

Politics makes strange bedfellows

Politics tends to bring together those who would normally avoid each other's company, and unlikely alliances may be forged for political reasons.

Possession is nine points of the law

A person who actually has something in his or her possession is in a strong position for claiming legal ownership of or entitlement to it.

Poverty comes from God, but not dirt

Some people cannot avoid being poor, but nobody has any excuse for being dirty or for failing to keep his or her house clean.

Poverty is no crime

The poor should not be despised.

Poverty waits at the gates of idleness

No work means no money.

Power corrupts, and absolute power corrupts absolutely

Power has an adverse effect on the integrity of those in authority, and the more power they have, the worse they become.

Practice makes perfect

It is believed that if one practices a certain skill often, he will excel in it

Practice what you preach

Follow the advice that you give to others.

Praise no man till he is dead

Final judgments on a person's qualities can only become reliable after he or she is dead.

Praise the bridge that carries you over

Do not criticize people or things that have helped you.

Prejudice is being down on what we are not up on

People automatically dislike or distrust anything they have no understanding of or familiarity with.

Prevention is better than cure

It is better to be careful beforehand than to try to solve a problem after it has arisen.

Pride feels no pain

People are able to endure or ignore the physical discomfort caused by smart or fashionable clothes, shoes, or jewelry; also used in other situations where people tolerate physical suffering in order not to lose face.

Pride goes before a fall

Arrogance and overconfidence often lead to humiliation or disaster; often used as a warning.

Procrastination is the thief of time

If you constantly put off doing things, you will only waste the time in which they could have been done and will ultimately run out of time in which to do them.

Promises, like piecrust, are made to be broken

People cannot be depended upon to keep their word.

Prosperity discovers vice; adversity, virtue

Wealth or good fortune often brings out the worst in a person, whereas hardship or misfortune brings out the best

Providence is always on the side of the big battalions

Those with the greatest strength, power, or influence always seem to have luck on their side and inevitably win the day.

Punctuality is the soul of business

Always be on time for everything.

Put a beggar on horseback, and he will ride to the devil

Sometimes, giving a person more than he needs or knows what to do with does not help him but instead, encourages him to go overboard.

Put your best foot forward

Always make the most of your strengths and abilities; also used to urge people to make their best effort or be on their best behavior.

Put your trust in God, and keep your powder dry

Do not pin all your hopes on divine assistance or intervention—always be prepared to take action yourself if necessary.

Q

Quickly come, quickly go

Something that arises suddenly is likely to disappear just as suddenly; also used of something that is rapidly gained and lost.

Quit while you are ahead

Give up doing something when you are in a good position rather than risk what you have already gained.

R

Rain before seven, fine before eleven

Rain early in the morning often heralds a fine day; occasionally applied to other things that start in an unpromising way.

Rats desert a sinking ship

When things go wrong in an organization, people tend to abandon it.

Render unto Caesar that which is Caesar's

Give what you have to give to those who have a better claim to them.

Repeating a life doesn't make it true

Saying something is true when it is not just because you would like to believe it is so does not change the facts.

Revenge is a dish best served cold

Revenge works well when the target least expects it.

Revenge is sweet

Some people feel good to be able to get back at someone who has hurt them.

Revolutions are not made with rose water

It is not possible to bring about drastic changes by pleasant, easy, or peaceful means, or without causing damage or suffering.

Riches have wings

Money is soon gone.

Robbing Peter to pay Paul

(this is quoted when one takes another loan to pay off an earlier loan) taking from one to give another.

Robin Hood could brave all weathers but a thaw wind

Of all kinds of weather, a raw wind after frost or snow is the most penetrating.

Rome was not built in a day

Any great plan or big dream cannot be achieved overnight or easily.

S

Safe bind, safe find

If you fasten things securely before you leave, or lock somebody or something away, they will still be there when you return:

Same meat, different gravy

The same thing presented differently.

Save me from my friends.

Sometimes some friends are more troublesome than enemies.

Save something for a rainy day

It is sensible to put money aside in case it is needed in the future.

Saying is one thing, doing is another

People don't always do what they say they'll do.

Scratch something and you'll find a something

When you know a person better, you will realize that he is not all he seems to be.

Second thoughts are best

Do not act on impulse.

See which way the wind is blowing

Test how things stand

Seek and ye shall find

When you set out to look for the truth with all your heart, you will find it

Seize the day

Live for the present, and take full advantage of every moment

Seldom seen, soon forgotten

Persons or things rarely seen or mentioned are quickly forgotten

Self trust is the first secret of success

You need to believe in your abilities first of all in order to succeed in life

Self-deceit is the easiest of any

It is easy to convince yourself of something that you want to believe:

Self-interest is the rule, self-sacrifice the exception

Most people are concerned about their own interests while it is only a few people who are selfless and giving.

Send a fool to market and a fool he'll return

A foolish person will always be foolish.

Set a thief to catch a thief

Use the skill and experience of one wrongdoer to catch another.

Short reckonings make long friends

Debts repaid quickly instigate friendships.

Shrouds have no pockets

Money is of no use to somebody after death.

Sickness in the body brings sadness to the mind.

Physical problems may lead to sadness.

Silence gives consent

If you do not protest, object or say anything in response to a proposal, plan etc. it means you are agreeable to it

Silence gives consent.

Not objecting to something means that you agree with it.

Sing before breakfast, cry before night

One who wakes up in the morning feeling happy tends to encounter sadness at the end of the day.

Six of one and half a dozen of the other

The same or nearly the same in one case as in the other

Slow and steady wins the race

Do things at your own pace and ability, and you will succeed in time

Small choice in rotten apples

It doesn't matter what you choose when faced with undesirable options.

Smile, and the world smiles with you; cry, and you cry alone

People are usually ready to share in your happiness but not in your sadness

Snug as a bug in a rug.

To feel very comfortable.

Soft and fair goes far

A calm and gentle attitude ensures that one achieves a lot.

Someone's bark is worse than his bite

Someone may seem frightening when they speak to us but they usually aren't as scary as they seem.

Something is better than nothing

Be thankful that you do have something, and do not complain about how little you have

Something is rotten in the state of denmark

something wrong or suspicious; refers to corruption.

Something that one already has is better than going after

something seemingly more worthwhile that one may not be able to get.

Soon ripe, soon rotten

premature success is short.

Spare and have is better than spend and crave

better to spend and save money wisely instead of wasting it and not having any when needed.

Spare at the spigot, and let out the bunghole

people who are reluctant to part with small sums of money are often careless and extravagant when spending on other things.

Spare the rod and spoil the child.

Not punishing a child when he commits something wrong will spoil his character.

Speak of the devil and he's sure to appear

What you say when you are talking of someone, and he appears

Speak softly and carry a big stick

Be peaceful when needed and forceful when needed.

Speak when you are spoken to

Respond when you are asked a question

Speech is silver, silence is golden

Talk may be beneficial, but sometimes acquiescence may be the best option to take.

Speech is silver, silence is golden

Sometimes discretion on something is better than speaking about it.

Starve a cold, feed a fever

The best way to treat a cold is to skip a meal or two; the best way to treat fever is to have a light meal.

Sticks and stones may break my bones but words will never hurt me

The unkind words of small-minded people should not upset or depress you.

Sticks and stones will break my bones but names will never hurt me.

Harsh words will not hurt me.

Still waters run deep

One who is usually silent and goes about his business quietly may be a very wise person.

Still waters run deep

A quiet and calm person is generally very wise.

Stolen fruit is the sweetest

Things that are forbidden to you seem to be the most exciting or tempting

Stolen pleasures are the sweetest.

Forbidden pleasures are the most tempting.

Stolen waters are sweet

pleasures gained through negative means are the most enjoyable.

Stone walls do not make a prison

thoughts cannot be restrained by physical elements.

Strike while the iron is hot

Seize a good opportunity as quickly as possible.

Success is a journey, not a destination

The most treasured part of an achievement is the experience and lessons you learn in the process.

Sufficient unto the day is the evil thereof

Do not be troubled about the problems you may face tomorrow, as you have enough to contend with today.

T

Take care of number one
one should take care of one's own interests before anybody else's interests.

Take care of the pence, and the pounds will take care of themselves
Pay attention to the details and the larger issues will work out well enough

Take the will for the deed
Take things as they come; deal with problems as they come.

Talk is cheap
Talk that is not backed up with action is useless

Tall oaks grow from little acorns
Small beginnings bring forth great results.

Tell not all you know, nor do all you can
Do not to reveal your complete knowledge.

Tell the truth and shame the devil
Tell the truth at all times

That government is best which governs least
The best form of government is one that allows people the greatest freedom.

That's where the shoe pinches
Referring to the source or cause of a problem.

The acorn never falls far from the tree
Children tend to resemble their parents

The apple doesn't fall far from the tree
Children resemble their parents.

The best advice is found on the pillow
A good night's sleep helps one find answers to one's problems.

The best art conceals art
Artistic excellence lies in making something that is subtle or intricate in construction appear simple and streamlined.

The best fish swim near the bottom
The best things are hard to come by.

The best is the enemy of the good.
By constantly striving for the best we risk destroying, or failing to produce, something good.

The best laid schemes of mice and men often fail
No matter how well planned, your arrangements can go wrong because you do not control all events and cannot see into the future.

The best of friends must part

Even good friends sometimes need to part, if only for a while

The best of men are but men at best

Even the greatest people have their failings and limitations.

The best things come in small packages

Size has no bearing on quality, and a small container may hold something of great value; often said by or to a short person.

The best things in life are free

The most rewarding or satisfying experiences in life are often those that cost nothing; also used of the wonders of nature or of abstract qualities such as health and friendship.

The bigger they are, the harder they fall

The bigger a problem the greater its impact

The biter is sometimes bit

Those who criticize or otherwise set about others are not immune from criticism or other attack themselves.

The blind leading the blind

A person helping or advising someone knows as little about the subject as the person who is being advised.

The buck stops here

It means final decision or total responsibility for an action

The busiest men have the most leisure.

People who are industrious by nature always seem to have the most spare time, either because they accomplish their work more quickly and efficiently or because they cram so much into their busy lives.

The calm comes before the storm

There is usually peace before disaster strikes

The cat would eat fish, but would not wet her feet

You must be prepared to put up with personal inconvenience, discomfort, or risk in order to get what you want; often used when somebody is hesitant about doing something for this reason.

The child is father of the man

A child's character is an indication of the type of adult he or she will become—human nature does not change from youth to maturity.

The clock goes as it pleases the clerk.

It is up to civil servants and other bureaucrats how time is governed and spent.

The company makes the feast

You will enjoy a meal or celebration far more if you are among cheerful friendly people, and the quality of the food and drink—or of the surroundings—is of lesser importance.

The cowl does not make the monk.

Do not judge a person's character by his or her outward appearance or behavior.

The cure is worse than the disease

Some solutions may be worse than the problem.

The customer is always right

The customer must be satisfied, so never upset or contradict a customer.

The danger past and God forgotten

People are prone to calling on God in times of trouble, only to forget all about their newly found religious faith as soon as the crisis is past.

The darkest hour is that before the dawn

Victory arrives after the worst phase of a bad situation is over.

The devil dances in an empty pocket

The poor are easily tempted to do evil.

The devil finds work for idle hands to do

Idle people may find themselves tempted into wrongdoing.

The devil has the best tunes

To do something unworthy because it gives you pleasure.

The devil is in the details

The details of something are of paramount importance, and you should always examine or pay attention to them in any proposition you are considering or any project you undertake.

The devil is not as black as he is painted

People are rarely as bad as others say they are; often used in defense of a specific person.

The devil looks after his own

Bad or undeserving people often prosper and thrive; said in response to the success or good fortune of such a person.

The devil was sick, the devil a saint would be; the devil was well, the devil a saint was he

People often turn to religion or promise to reform when they are ill or in trouble, only to revert to their former ways as soon as the crisis is over.

The difficult is done at once, the impossible takes a little longer

Difficult tasks present no problem, and even those that seem impossible will ultimately be accomplished; used as a motto or policy statement, as in commerce.

The dog always returns to his vomit

People always return to the scene of their crime or wrongdoing.

The dogs bark, but the caravan goes on

The warnings or protests of those in lowly positions are often ignored by those in power and are not allowed to stand in the way of progress.

The early bird catches the worm.

If you want to do something successfully, you should do it as soon as you can.

The end justifies the means

Any course of action, however immoral or unscrupulous, is justifiable if it achieves a worthy objective.

The exception proves the rule

The existence of an exception to a rule shows that the rule itself exists and is applicable in other cases; often used loosely to explain away any such inconsistency.

The eyes are the window of the soul

A person's eyes express his/her true feelings and thoughts etc.

The fat is in the fire

Said when it is too late to improve a situation.

The female of the species is deadlier than the male

Women often prove to be more dangerous than men, when roused to anger.

The first hundred years are the hardest

Life will always be difficult.

The first step is the hardest

The beginning is the most difficult phase of a situation.

The first step is the hardest

The most difficult thing is to begin.

The first step to health is to know that we are sick

One should admit that there is a problem before one remedies it.

The game is not worth the candle.

It is not worth persisting in an enterprise that is unlikely to yield enough profit or benefit to compensate for the effort or expense involved, or that carries a risk, actual harm or loss.

The gods send nuts to those who have no teeth

Opportunities or good fortune often come too late in life for people to enjoy them or take full advantage of them; also applied more generally to people of any age who are unable to use or benefit from good things that come their way.

The golden age was never the present age

The past and the future always seem infinitely preferable to the present time.

The gray mare is the better horse.

A woman is often more competent or powerful than a man; used specifically of wives who have the upper hand over their husbands.

The greater the truth, the greater the libel

Some people will take greater offense at a true accusation of wrongdoing than at a false one.

The hand that rocks the cradle rules the world

Mothers have a powerful influence—if indirectly—on world affairs, because it is they who mold the characters of future leaders.

The head and feet keep warm, the rest will take no harm

Take care of the important matters and everything else will fall into place.

The higher the monkey climbs the more he shows his tail.

People's faults and shortcomings become increasingly obvious as they advance to positions of high office.

The highest branch is not the safest roost

Those in the highest positions of power or authority are, in some respects, the most vulnerable, because there will always be plenty of others eager to take their place or cause their downfall.

The hole calls the thief

Criminals and other wrong-doers will go where opportunity presents itself.

The house shows the owner

A person's character is revealed by the state of his or her house.

The journey is the reward

The work and effort put into a job is the most fulfilling part of the job.

The king can do no wrong

People in authority are not bound by the rules and regulations that apply to others; specifically, a monarch is above the law.

The laborer is worthy of his hire

Those who work for others are entitled to be paid for their efforts.

The last drop makes the cup run over

One final additional thing may push a person beyond his or her limit of tolerance or endurance.

The last straw that broke the camel's back

Refers to the last thing that is added to existing problems which can ruin everything without any scope for improvement.

The least said, the soonest mended

Talk less during a quarrel and you'll fix it sooner.

The lion is not so fierce as he is painted

Some people have reputations that far exceed their real characters.

The longest day must have an end

All difficult jobs or situations also have an end.

The longest mile is the last mile home

The nearer one is to one's destination the farther it seems.

The longest way around is the shortest way home.

It is best to do things carefully and thoroughly rather than trying to cut corners.

The man who is born in a stable is not a horse

A person does not necessarily have the stereotypical characteristics of the place where he or she was born.

The meek shall inherit the earth

Humane people are the ones who are rewarded.

The more acquaintance, the more danger

There is a greater chance of going on the wrong path if one has many casual friends.

The more haste, the less speed

A person makes more progress if they take time to do things carefully.

The more one knows, the less one believes

The more information one has about something the more suspicious one becomes about it.

The more you get, the more you want

Greediness makes one want more even though one already has a lot.

The more you have, the more you want.

People have a constant desire to possess more.

The more you know, the more you know you don't know

The more knowledge one receives, the more aware one becomes about how little one knows about life.

The more you stir it, the worse it stinks

The more you investigate an dubious affair, the more unpleasant details you discover.

The mother of mischief is no bigger than a midge's wing

A great quarrel, or other major trouble, is often caused by something trivial

The mountain labors and brings forth a mouse

Refers to a situation where one has worked hard on a project, for a long time but then all the effort goes in vain.

The mouse that has but one hole is quickly taken

One should have alternatives because having one solution puts one at a risk of losing that too.

The nail that sticks out gets pounded

People who are different from the people in their peer group are generally pressurised into conforming to the group's general dynamics.

The nearer the bone, the sweeter the meat/flesh

The closer one is to one's goal, the more happy one gets.

The nearer the church, the farther from God

People who are active members or officials of a church are often the least godly in their daily lives; also applied to those who live close to a church.

The obvious choice is usually a quick regret

Think carefully before you make a selection or decision.

The only free cheese is in the mouse trap

It is better to be careful in accepting free things because it may be a trap.

The only stupid question is the one that is not asked

Do not hold back in knowing more about something. The more one asks the more knowledge one gains.

The only thing a heated argument ever produced is coolness

An angry exchange of words resolves nothing and leads to a breakdown of friendly relations.

The opera ain't over till the fat lady sings

Wait until something finally comes to an end before you give up hope, celebrate your success, abandon your efforts, or make a judgment.

The pen is mightier than the sword

Words and communication have greater effect than war and fighting.

The pitcher will go to the well once too often

Nothing can continue or be repeated indefinitely—a run of good fortune or success must come to an end, persistent cheats or swindlers will ultimately be caught out.

The post of honor is the post of danger

The most perilous positions in an administration or organization are those that have the highest prestige.

The price of liberty is eternal vigilance

Freedom can only be preserved by keeping a watch on any threat to it.

The proof of the pudding is in the eating

To know how good something is one has to test it.

The proof of the pudding is in the eating

The real value of something can be judged only after it has been tried or tested.

The race is not to the swift, nor the battle to the strong

Speed and power do not guarantee success—those who are slower and weaker may win through perseverance or tactics.

The rain falls on the just and the unjust alike

one has to face everyday problems regardless of being good or bad.

The rich man has his ice in the summer and the poor man gets his in the winter

It may seem that everybody, rich or poor, has an equal share of good fortune in life, but this is not so.

The road to hell is paved with good intentions

Good intentions don't guarantee success.

The road to hell is paved with good intentions

It's not enough to intend to do something, you must actually do it.

The sharper the storm, the sooner it's over

The most uncomfortable situation will last the least amount of time.

The shoe is on the other foot

To say that a situation has been reversed.

The shoemaker's child always goes barefoot

Eople generally don't benefit from the professional skills of their close ones.

The show must go on

Meaning that things must continue as they are even if there is a risk of something going wrong.

The sins of the fathers will be visited upon the children

Children may have to face the consequences of wrongdoings committed by their parents, grandparents etc.

The sky is the limit

There is no upper limit to something.

The spirit is willing but the flesh is weak

To do something disgraceful only because it gives one pleasure.

The start of a journey should never be mistaken for success

Don't mistake yourself to be successful at something when you have just started with it.

The sun loses nothing by shining into a puddle

One who is truly good natured will not be corrupted by negative elements.

The thread breaks where it is weakest

A weak point in a thread or anything else is likely to be the point where the whole thing fails.

The tongue always returns to the sore tooth

People cannot help thinking or talking about what is bothering them most at a particular time.

The tongue wounds more than a lance

Insults can be more hurtful than physical injuries.

The tree is known by its fruit

People should judged by what they do or produce—specifically, by their children—rather than by first impressions or outward appearance.

The truth hurts

The truth can be harsh sometimes when one has believed something else to be true.

The truth is in the wine

People speak more freely under the influence of alcohol.

The truth will out

Truth about something will eventually be discovered or made known

The used key is always bright

Activity, work, and exercise keep the mind and body in good form.

The voice of the people is the voice of

God The will of the people must be obeyed; also used to imply that the people are always right.

The way to a man's heart is though his stomach.

If you feed a man well, he will love you.

The way to a man's heart is through his stomach

Feed a man well and he will love you.

The weak can never forgive.

Only those who are morally strong have the capability to forgive.

The weakest go to the wall

In any conflict or struggle, the weakest will always lose, be defeated, fail, or be ruined.

The wearer best knows where the shoe pinches

Nobody can fully understand another person's hardship or suffering.

The wheel comes full circle

Happenings move about in such a manner than they seem to reach the beginning after some time thereby making a circle of events.

The wheel of fortune is forever in motion

Meaning that people's fortunes are constantly changing.

The wish is father to the thought

What one wishes for is what one eventually acts upon.

The wish is father to the thought.

Something is thought to be true because one wants it to be true.

The wish is father to the thought

You think that something is true because you want it to be so.

The young cock crows as he heard the old one

The young learn by the example of their elders.

The youth must be served

Young people should be allowed to have their own way.

Thee is no venom like that of the tongue

The cruel things people sometimes say to one another can hurt more than the deadliest poison can

There are only twenty-four hours in a day

Time is limited, use it wisely.

There are no endings, only new beginnings

The end of something is not actually the, but the beginning of something else.

There are no small parts, only small actors

A good actor will make any role interesting, regardless of it being small or big.

There are none so blind as those that will not see

People who don't admit that they are wrong, don't listen to others' opinions.

There are none so deaf as those who will not hear

People will hear only what they want to hear.

There are other fish in the sea

Plenty more people, things, opportunities, or options are available; often used to console somebody whose relationship with a boyfriend or girlfriend has ended.

There are two sides to every question

There are always two perceptions of anything.

There is a black sheep in every flock

There is always one person in the group who is different from the others.

There is a trick in every trade

There is a specific and fixed way of doing things.

There is many at a true word that is spoken in jest

Something said humorously about someone may in fact be true about that person.

There is no fool like an old fool

An older person is expected to behave more sensibly.

There is no honor among thieves

Nobody can trust thieves.

There is no place like home

Even a simple home is the best place in the world for the people who live in it.

There is no point arguing with the barrel of a gun

It is pointless trying to argue with a very angry person.

There is no such thing as a free lunch

Nothing is free.

There is nothing new under the sun

There is nothing in the world that has not been seen, heard, discovered, experienced before.

There is one law for the rich, and another for the poor

When the law is unjust and does not treat people fairly, but considers their wealth and status before deciding to help them.

There is safety in numbers

You are safer when others are around.

There'll be sleeping enough in the grave

Life is too short to waste time having more sleep than you need.

There's a pot of gold at the end of the rainbow

Some things can never be achieved; used when people chase after ideals or ambitions that constantly elude them.

There's a sin of omission as well as of commission

There are times when failure to do what you should is as bad as doing what you should not do.

There's a skeleton in every closet

Every person, family, or organization has a shameful secret.

There's luck in leisure

It is better not to act in haste; sometimes used to justify procrastination.

There's many a good cock come out of a tattered bag

Do not be misled by external appearances.

It is what is inside or what emerges from something that counts

Also used to imply that people should not be judged by their parents, clothes, or background

There's many a good tune played on an old fiddle

Old people should not be dismissed as incapable.

There's measure in all things

Everything should be done in moderation.

There's no disputing about tastes

There is no point in arguing about what is good or bad, since everybody likes different things.

There's no royal road to learning

Knowledge and skills can only be acquired by hard work—there are no short cuts.

There's no smoke without fire

Rumors usually have a factual basis, although they may present a misleading or exaggerated version of the truth.

There's no such thing as bad weather, only the wrong clothes

Any weather is tolerable if you are suitably dressed for it.

There's nothing new under the sun

What is thought to be a novelty is often shown to be nothing more than a revival or reintroduction of an old idea; also used as a comment on the changeless nature of things.

There's nothing so good for the inside of a man as the outside of a horse

Riding is a healthy pastime.

There's no smoke without fire

Rumors do not spread unless there is some element of truth in them.

They also serve who only stand and wait

You can be often be helpful without actively doing anything; also used to commend or encourage patience and endurance

They that dance must pay the piper

Those who gain pleasure or benefit from something must be prepared to bear the costs or suffer the consequences.

They that sow the wind shall reap the whirlwind

People who provoke trouble or violence—or behave in a reckless manner—will suffer far worse consequences.

They who dance must pay the fiddler

You must be ready to accept the consequences of your actions

Things come in threes

According to popular superstition, two similar occurrences—bad or good—are inevitably followed by a third.

Things past cannot be recalled

It is too late for regret after something is done sometimes used to advise caution.

Think before you speak

Think before you say anything so that you do not say something foolish or hurtful

Think much, speak little, and write less

It is best to think long and hard about something before expressing any thoughts about it.

Thinking is very far from knowing

Opinion and conjecture are not the same as knowledge and certainty.

This, too, shall pass

Do not despair—an unpleasant situation or a difficult period will not last forever.

Those who can, do; those who can't,teach

People who are incapable of putting their knowledge and skills to practical use go into education.

Those who cannot remember the past are condemned to repeat it

Those who forget, are ignorant of, or fail to learn from the mistakes of earlier generations are likely to make the same mistakes themselves.

Those who hide can find

The person who finds something is often the person who hid it in the first place.

Those who know don't speak; those who speak don't know

Those who talk the most volubly are usually those who know the least about the subject in question

Those who live in glass houses should not throw stones

People with obvious faults should not criticse the faults of others because they are themselves targets for criticism

Those who play at bowls must look out for rubbers

It is foolish to embark on or participate in an enterprise without being aware of or taking account of the problems you may encounter.

Thought is free

Anybody may think whatever he or she likes.

Threatened men live long

Threats are often not carried out, and people who have been warned are on their guard and therefore in less danger than others; sometimes said in defiant response to a threat or warning.

Three may keep a secret, if two of them are dead

It is impossible for two or more people to keep a secret.

Thrift is a great revenue

Saving and frugality lead to financial gain.

Throw dirt enough, and some will stick

A reputation that is constantly attacked cannot remain undamaged—if false accusations or defamatory remarks are repeated often enough, people will begin to believe them.

Throw out a sprat to catch a mackerel

It is worth making a small sacrifice to gain something of much greater value.

Time and tide wait for no one

Time is precious, once it is past no one can go back and claim it thus everyone should be mindful of how his time is spent.

Time cures all things

With time, people are likely to forgive and forget hurts.

Time flies

Time seems to move very fast when you are having fun or doing something urgent.

Time hangs heavy on idle hands

Time seems to pass more slowly when we have little or nothing to do.

Time has wings

Time goes by quickly.

Time heals all wounds

The passage of time lessens the impact of bad events.

Time is a great healer

Time allows people to forgive and forget past hurts, injuries and loss as memories fade, and people become wiser and more mature.

Time is money

Time is valuable and should not be wasted.

Time is the rider that breaks youth

Young people become less wild and more sensible with age.

Time the deed to the need

Help should be given only when required.

Times change, and we with time

Customs, values, and circumstances are constantly changing, and we must adapt ourselves accordingly.

To accuse the times is but excusing ourselves

To accuse one's environment and timing rather than oneself.

To each his own

Everybody has his or her own tastes and idiosyncrasies.

To err is human, to forgive divine

It is only normal for man to make mistakes and do wrong, but for one to forgive another for his wrong is indeed great and gracious act.

To the pure all things are pure

Virtuous people tend to be unaware of the wickedness or evil that is around them; sometimes used to imply naivety.

To the victor belong the spoils

The winner of a contest or battle gets everything that goes with victory:

To understand all is to forgive all

One can forgive a person for what he/she does if one understands that person's reasons do that particular act.

Today is yesterday's tomorrow

You cannot go on putting things off, because the future becomes the present.

Today you, tomorrow me

What happens to one person one day could happen to another person the next day.

Tomorrow is another day

Don't worry about what has happened today—things may improve tomorrow; also used in reference to making a fresh start.

Tomorrow never comes

One should do what one has to do, today itself and not tomorrow.

Too many chiefs and not enough Indians

There are too many people giving orders and not enough following them, or too many people in charge and not enough to do the work.

Too many cooks spoil the broth

Too many people trying to help can be a hindrance; also used of too many people working on the same project, often pulling in different directions.

Too many cooks spoil the broth

Too many people doing the same thing at the same time will lead to disaster.

Too much bed makes a dull head.

Too much sleep leads to difficulty in thinking.

Toot your own horn lest the same be never tooted

Sing your own praises, in case nobody else does.

Touch wood

If nothing goes wrong, everything will turn out satisfactorily.

Trade follows the flag

One nation may colonize another for commercial purposes.

Travel broadens the mind

People become more broad-minded and knowledgeable by visiting other countries and learning about the customs, culture, and lifestyle of those who live there.

Trifles make perfection, and perfection is no trifle

Perfection is a great thing, but not easy to achieve, and attention to detail is of the utmost importance.

True blue will never stain

Persons of real integrity can never be corrupted.

Trust everybody, but cut the cards

Have faith in the honesty and integrity of those around you, but remain on your guard and take precautions in case you are wrong.

Trust not a horse's heel nor a dog's tooth

A horse kicks from behind, a dog attacks with its teeth.

Trust not a horse's heel nor a dog's tooth

A horse kicks from behind, a dog attacks with its teeth.

Trust not a new friend nor an old enemy

It is foolish to trust either a friend of short standing or someone else who may harbor hostile feelings.

Trust not one night's ice

Do not rely upon something that has yet to be tried and tested.

Truth has no answer

You cannot argue against facts or refute what is true.

Truth is stranger than fiction

Events in real life are often stranger than in fiction.

Truth is the first casualty of war

When war breaks out, the truth quickly succumbs to propaganda and rumor.

Truth is truth to the end of the reckoning

The truth can never be changed:

Truth lies at the bottom of a well

It is often very difficult to discover the truth.

Try not to become a man of success but a man of value

A moral and good character matter more than success.

Turn up like a bad penny

Something or someone disliked just won't go away

Two boys are half a boy, and three boys are no boy at all

When two or more boys work together, they distract each other and do less work between them than a single boy working alone.

Two heads are better than one

It is always better to get the view of another than to rely entirely on one's own judgment.

Two of a trade never agree

Members of the same trade or profession often do not get on with one another, because of rivalry.

Two things prolong your life: a quiet heart and a loving wife

Inner peace and a dependable life partner ensure that one has a good life.

Two wrongs do not make a right

If a person does something to harm or offend us, that's wrong. If we do something to harm them back, that's wrong too.

Two's company, three's a crowd

Refers to two person's quality time with each other being disrupted by a third unwanted person.

U,V

Uneasy lies the head that wears a crown

Those in power are weighed down by responsibilities, feelings of insecurity, or fears of losing their position and can never rest easy.

Union is strength

A group has more force than an individual.

United we stand, divided we fall

Individual strength does not stand any chance of winning against unity.

Unity is strength

Unity makes a group or a time strong.

Unwillingness easily finds an excuse

A person who doesn't want to do something always finds a reason to avoid it.

Use legs and have legs

The body, among other things, will continue to work properly only if kept in regular use.

Variety is the spice of life

Change and difference make life interesting.

Virtue is its own reward

If one has good moral values one should not expect to be rewarded for that because morality should be self-imbibed.

Walls have ears, shoes have tongues
One should be careful about what one says and who one speaks to.

Walls have ears
Be careful. People could be listening.

Walnuts and pears you plant for your heirs
Walnut trees and pear trees take a long time to produce fruit.

Wanton kittens make sober cats
People who live wildly or extravagantly in their youth usually develop into sensible and responsible adults.

War is too important to be left to the generals
Those in authority cannot be relied on to do their job properly; applied to warfare, diplomacy, or government.

War will cease when men refuse to fight
There will always be war while there are people who are prepared to serve in the armed forces; a pacifist slogan.

Waste not, want not
If you make full and careful use of your resources, you will never be in need; applied to everything from the eating up of leftover food to domestic and industrial recycling.

Waste not, want not
If you never waste anything, you will have it when you need it.

Water is the only drink for a wise Man *Wise people avoid drinking alcohol.*

Water seeks its own level
People tend to be drawn toward, or to end up with, others of the same background, class, intelligence, or experience.

We all have our cross to bear
Nobody is exempt from suffering—we all have our own problems and afflictions.

We must eat a peck of dirt before we die
Everybody must suffer a certain amount of unpleasantness during his or her lifetime; also used literally, as when eating unwashed food.

We must learn to walk before we can run
It is necessary to learn the basics before progressing to more advanced things.

We never miss the water till the well runs dry
One only realizes the importance of something/one when it/they is/are gone.

Wealth makes many friends
Many people want to be the friend of a rich person.

Wear out one's welcome
One is no longer welcome, usually because he has become a nuisance

Wear your learning like your watch, in a private pocket
Do not make a show of your knowledge or education.

Wedlock is a padlock
Marriage puts many restrictions on a person's freedom.

Welcome is the best cheer
Welcoming your guests with friendly hospitality is more important than giving them fine food.

What a man says drunk, he thinks sober
People speak more freely under the influence of alcohol.

What a man says drunk, he thinks sober
People speak more freely under the influence of alcohol.

What a tangled web we weave when first we practice to deceive
Once you have told one lie, you find yourself supporting it with other related lies, constructing an elaborate network of deceit from which it is not easy to escape.

What can you expect from a pig but a grunt
Boorish or uncouth people cannot be expected to behave in any other way; used as an insult when such a person says or does something rude.

What can't be cured must be endured
If something cannot be put right, we must learn to put up with it.

What goes around, comes around
How one treats others is how one will be treated by others later on.

What has happened once can happen again
Something that has a precedent cannot be dismissed as impossible, and may recur.

What is learnt in the cradle lasts to the tomb
All lessons learnt in life stay with one till death.

What is sauce for the goose is sauce for the gander
Something that is good for one person will be good for another person as well.

What the eye doesn't see, the heart doesn't grieve over
If one doesn't know about something one cannot feel sad about it.

What the eye doesn't see, the heart doesn't grieve over
If a person doesn't know about something, it cannot hurt them.

What the eye doesn't see, the heart doesn't grieve over
If a person doesn't know about something, it cannot hurt them.

What the soldier said isn't evidence
Gossip and rumour cannot be taken as the truth.

What will be, will be
what has to happen will happen.

What you don't know can't hurt you
It is better to ignore things that could sadden you.

What you lose on the swings you gain on the roundabouts
Disadvantages suffered in one place are nullified by advantages won in another place.

What you sow is what you reap
Face the consequences of one's actions.

What you've never had you never miss
You do not feel the lack of something you have never possessed.

What's bred in the bone will come out in the flesh
A new generation will reflect characteristics of the older one.

What's got over the devil's back is spent under his belly
Money acquired through immoral means is spent in a similar manner.

What's new cannot be true
To be sceptical about new ideas.

What's past is prologue
Old happenings are an introduction to future events.

What's yours is mine, and what's mine is my own
People want to use others' stuff but refuse to share their own possessions.

Whatever man has done, man may do
If one person has succeeded in doing something, it should not be impossible for another person to do it too.

What's done can't be undone
In life there are some things once done or decisions once made cannot be changed; malicious words once uttered or harmful actions once done cannot be taken back.

When a dog bites a man, that is not news; but when a man bites a dog, that is news
The media is only interested in covering unusual stories.

When all fruit fails, welcome haws
One must accept whatever is available.

When all you have is a hammer, everything looks like a nail
People who aren't very smart tend to use the same options to solve all problems.

When Greek meets Greek, then comes the tug of war
A contest or struggle between equally matched opponents is a long and fierce battle.

When house and land are gone and spent, then learning is most excellent
It is important to have a good education to fall back on if you lose or use up all your money and material assets.

When in doubt, do nothing
If you are unsure what to do, it is best to do nothing at all.

When in Rome do as the Romans do
When one is in a new place, country or situation he must adapt himself to the new manners and customs.

When one sows the wind one reaps the whirlwind
If one lives a fast-paced life, one is bound to face difficulties.

When poverty comes in at the door, love flies out of the window
Financial problems can cause the breakdown of a marriage or other relationships.

When the cat's away, the mice will play
People do as they please in the absence of those in authority.

When the going gets tough, the tough get going
Strong people work harder when faced with difficult situations.

When thieves fall out, honest men come by their own
A dispute between criminals is to the advantage of their victims, either because they betray one another and reveal the truth, or because they are too busy arguing to commit the crime in the first place.

When you are in a hole, stop digging
When you have landed yourself in trouble, such as through a foolish remark or action, do not say or do anything to make the situation worse.

When you argue with a fool, make sure he isn't doing the something
Do not assume that you are more intelligent or knowledgeable than the person you are arguing with.

When you go to dance, take heed whom you take by the hand
Beware of getting involved with dishonest or unscrupulous people.

Where bees are, there is honey
Wherever there are industrious people, wealth is produced; (also used of other types of people whose presence is indicative or suggestive of something).

Where God builds a church, the devil will build a chapel
Any force for good, such as progress or reform, is inevitably accompanied—or closely followed— by something bad; not exclusively used in religious contexts.

Where the carcass is, there will the eagles be gathered
People are drawn together, or
to a particular place, when they think they will gain something to their advantage.*

Where there's no vision, the people perish
People need hopes and dreams to sustain themselves.

Where there's a will there's a way
When a person really wants to do something, he will find a way of doing it.

Where there's life there's hope
As long as a person is breathing, there is hope for recovery.

Which came first, the chicken or the egg?
It is sometimes difficult to distinguish between cause and effect.

While the grass grows, the steed starves
If somebody has to wait a long time for something, it may arrive too late to be of use.

While two dogs are fighting for a bone, a third runs away with it
When two parties are engaged in a dispute, their attention is distracted from what is going on around them, and both may end up as losers.

Whiskey and gasoline don't mix
Do not drive an automobile after drinking alcohol.

Who has land has war
There will always be disputes over the ownership of land.

Who keeps company with wolves, will learn to howl
If we associate with bad companions we, too, will become bad

Who makes himself a sheep will be eaten by the wolves
Possible interpretation: an easily influenced person can be mislead.

Who repairs not his gutters repairs his whole house

Those who neglect small repairs will find they have to make much bigger ones later.

Who says A must say B

If you say or do one thing, you must be prepared to say or do what logically follows.

Whom the gods would destroy, they first make mad

Those who commit acts of great folly are heading for disaster, the implication being that such people lose their sanity or good sense because they are destined for this end.

Whose bread I eat, his song I sing

People show loyalty to, or comply with the demands of, those who employ, pay, or feed them.

Wilful waste makes woeful want

Do not waste anything that you may require later.

Winning isn't everything

The journey of becoming victorious is more important than victory itself.

Wisdom is better than strength

It is preferable to use one's intelligence than one's physical strength.

Wonders will never cease!

Expressing surprise at an unexpected pleasure or event.

Worry often gives a small thing a big shadow

Worrying over small details can make them seem worse.

Y,Z

You are never too old to learn
You can always learn something new, no matter how old you are.

You are what you eat
What you eat has an effect on your well-being.

You can lead a horse to water but you can't make him drink
We can help, show or encourage someone to do something but we can't make him do what he is unwilling or unable to do.

You can't make bricks without straw
You cannot produce anything without the necessary materials or resources.

You can't put a square peg in a round hole
Do not give somebody a job for which he or she is unsuited or unqualified; also used of other situations in which a person is a misfit.

You can't put an old head on young shoulders
It is unreasonable to expect young people to be as sensible or knowledgeable as their elders.

You can't put new wine in old bottles
The introduction of new methods, ideas, items, or components into something old and well established—

or old and decrepit—*can have disastrous consequences.*

You can't run with the hare and hunt with the hounds
You cannot support two opposing parties at the same time.

You can't serve God and mammon
A devout or virtuous way of life is incompatible with the pursuit of material wealth and possessions.

You can't shift an old tree without it dying
Relocation is not good for old people.

You can't step twice into the same river
Things are constantly changing.

You can't take it with you
You might as well spend your money while you are alive, because it can't be carried with you into the next world.

You can't unscramble eggs
Wrongdoings cannot be undone.

You can't win 'em all
One can't achieve everything.

You cannot make a silk purse out of a sow's ear
You cannot change a person's real character.

You can't have it both ways
You can't be neutral in every

situation; you have to make a choice.

You can't have your cake and eat it
You can't have two things at the same time.

You can't make an omelette without breaking the eggs
Something has to be sacrificed so as to obtain something else.

You can't please everyone
One cannot make everyone around oneself happy.

You can't shoe a running horse
Help will be given only if one asks for it.

You can't teach an old dog new tricks
A person who is used to doing things a certain way cannot change.

You could go a lot further and fare a lot worse
Things could be worse, instead you are in a good situation now.

You have to take the rough with the smooth
Everything has pleasant and unpleasant—or difficult and easy—aspects

You need to bait the hook to catch the fish
One needs to plan and prepare before one can do anything.

You never know what you can do until you try
People are often surprised to discover what they are capable of when they make an effort.

You pay your money and you take your choice
It is one's own choice what one wants to do.

You pay your money and you take your chances
A humorous way of saying that we sometimes must trust in luck when buying something.

You scratch my back and I'll scratch yours
You help me and I'll help you.

You should know a man seven years before you stir his fire
You should not be too familiar with people until you have known them for some time.

You snooze, you lose
Those who fail to keep alert will lose out.

You will never know till you have tried it
To know and judge something one has to experience it.

You win some, you lose some
Winning and losing are a part of life; you cannot expect to win every situation.

Young folks think old folks to be fools, but old folks know young folks to be fools
Young people think they are wiser than their elders, but it is the opposite which is true.

Young men may die, but old men must die
Death is a possibility at any age, but a certainty in old age.

Young saint, old devil
Those who behave best when they are young are often those who behave worst when they are old.

Youth and age will never agree
The young and the old usually don't agree on various topics.

Youth will have its fling
Young people should be forgiven for their excesses or improprieties.

Zeal without knowledge is a runaway horse
Uninformed enthusiasm will only lead to disaster.

www.ingramcontent.com/pod-product-compliance
Lightning Source LLC
Chambersburg PA
CBHW070913030726
47504CB00005B/1573